KARSTEN KREPINSKY

The Attack Of The ISombies

Episode 1: They've Come To Turn You

Translated from the German by
KARIN DUFNER

Copyright © 2015 by Karsten Krepinsky
English translation in 2021 by Karin Dufner
www.karindufner.de
First published with the title Angriff der ISombies by
Karsten Krepinsky/Neuwelt Verlag.
Cover design by Ingo Krepinsky, Die TYPONAUTEN
www.typonauten.de/eng
Printed and published by BoD – Books on Demand,
Norderstedt
ISBN: 9783755737025

www.karstenkrepinsky.de

About this Book

Zombies have launched an attack on Berlin, slaughtering anyone who gets in their way. While politicians run for cover, a mismatched group of young outcasts stands up to the challenge...

Absolutely non-PC. A subversive Zombie satire.

Warning!

Reading this Zombie Apocalypse might trigger PC anxiety in sensitive people, making comprehensive brain restructuring surgery unavoidable.

For people who don't go with the flow.

You should recognize them by their deeds, not by their words.
1. John 2, 1-6

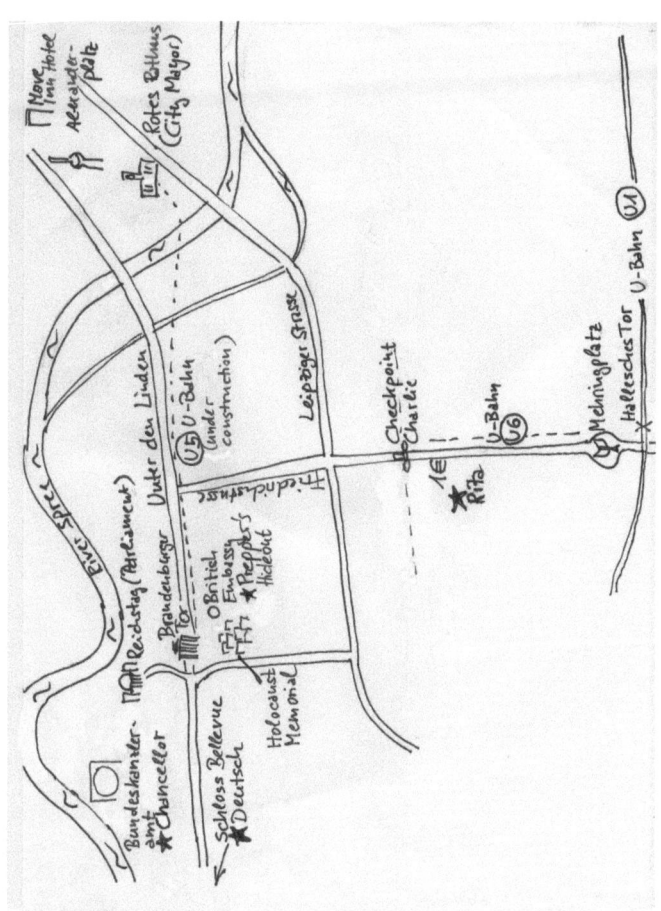

Map of Berlin

1.

The fire of loathing is burning hot inside me when I direct my steps toward the awe-inspiring stone structure—the heart of a country that once was my country, too. Something is driving my twitching body onward with the irresistible urge to sink my teeth into human flesh. The national flag is blowing in the wind. Sunlight, reflected in a dome of glass. Wisps of smoke, spiraling high into the skies. My mind has finally given up trying to control my body. It was a hard struggle, but in the end a higher power won out. I now know that I can turn them all. I'm nothing but a vessel, destined to pass on the seed I carry inside of me. For the rise of a new society. "To the German People" I read the inscription above the entrance portal, before my senses finally take leave of me and the parasites grabs hold of the wheel.

2.

One day earlier
Berlin, September 24
Schloss Bellevue, Office of the President of the Federal Republik of Germany

President Deutsch sat at his desk, golden fountain pen in hand, having just deleted the last sentence he had written.

~~Globalization is a chance, albeit a choice wrought with risks.~~

Somehow this didn't sound like the right beginning of a ground-breaking speech, meant to secure him a place in the history books. He knew what was at stake, of course, during this fateful epoch his country was going through. Therefore, this speech needed to be nothing less but his legacy to his people. It simply had to leave a lasting impression, following in the tradition of his otherwise rather unlucky predecessor, whose casual remark about the new import-religion in this country had made some waves. Not an easy feat, the President thought, as the Chancellor had even gone a step further by refusing to set a limit for the number of asylum-seekers allowed in. What was left for Deutsch to say to make him the darling of the press and entice those journos to sing his praise as the intellectual and humanist he aspired to be? He stood, planted his palms on the desk, struck a position befitting a head of state, and presented his less-than-aquiline three-quarter view to the gilded mirror. The intercom buzzed and his secretary announced that his Undersecretary, Michael Mustermann, wished to see him. Why not? the President thought with a complacent smile, pressing the intercom button. "Just show him in." Maybe his flunky would come up with a brilliant suggestion for his speech.

Mustermann stopped in the door with a slight bow and then proceeded toward the desk in an unusual hasty manner. "We need to evacuate Bellevue at once," he burst out, his voice shrill, yes, almost hysterical. One hand fumbled, testing the state of his comb-over.

"What?" the president asked, sounding less surprised than annoyed due to his lackey's strident tones.

"There's fighting in Kreuzberg and Wedding."

"Fighting? What are you talking about? A Russian invasion?"

"The helicopter is scheduled to land in the yard in ten minutes sharp," Mustermann ignored his superior's question.

"But... now is not... and what about our annual reception for the members of the press? You must be joking, old boy."

"The reception has to... it can't... I... I don't see any other option."

The President touched his index finger to his lip. "And if we moved the reception to Bonn?" he asked with a wide smile, looking proud as if expecting applause for his presence of mind.

"The helicopter. Don't you see?" Mustermann insisted.

The President waved him off. "A man is bound to his duties even in turbulent times, and you are surely aware of what a President's duties entail. He is the Representative of his country. And therefore it has to be our foremost priority having Werner come here at once," Deutsch chided Mustermann. "A great photographer, this man," he added. "He did fabulous portraits of me at the last reception. From the front upward and with a slight angle." The President proceeded to admire his own reflection in the mirror. "I even took up ballroom-dancing to raise to the occasion. No one will steal my show this time. And, by the way, the President of the United States has set aside half an hour just for me alone. I've looked up the protocols: No American leader ever has spent so much time with his German counterpart."

"But the helicopter..." Mustermann almost lost control over his features, a lapse which, however, was made impossible by the fact, that his facial repertoire only made two variants available. The dozens of muscles, shaping the human face into the different expressions that reflected a person's state of mind, just seemed to have two versions on stock. Number one, employed whenever Mustermann felt nervous, under attack, or genuinely happy—or also while professing love to his wife, an incident that, in all likelihood, hadn't occurred for the last two decades – resembled an inane failing-to-be-ironic grin. Number two could have been mistaken for the shocked stare of a schoolboy who had just been caught cheating during an exam. The last time the world had been exposed to variant number two was four years ago when Mustermann's party had awarded him with the position of Undersecretary.

"Keep your hair on, old boy." The President's laugh turned into a little cough. "The bird won't take off without me." He walked around his desk and put a hand on his Undersecretary's shoulder. "Why don't you start packing my personal things?"

"Yes, sir," Mustermann said with a subservient bow.

"I'll go ahead to the helicopter," Deutsch continued, his lips pursed, walking out of his office with measured steps and only speeding up after he could be sure that Mustermann wasn't watching. Mustermann picked up the briefcase from under the floor lamp and hurried over to the desk, where he started to empty the first top drawers. On a final note he also stuffed a tube of hair gel and both combs into the case. When he walked out of the office, the secretary at the front desk had already left. Making his way through the empty corridors of Schloss Bellevue, he heard nothing but the hollow sound of his footsteps. He found it odd, that there was no one waiting for him. He pushed through the double front doors, where the helicopter was parked in the middle of a flower bed, its rotor already in motion.

"Your things!" Mustermann called, holding out the case. But the pilot ignored him, revving up the engine, and soon the helicopter was airborne. While Mustermann slowly came down the front steps, the machine soared up into the sky. An armored government car shot down the gravel path crossing the grounds of Bellevue, raced out into the street, and disappeared, tires squealing, in the direction of Tiergarten. Soon, there was nobody left but a lone gardener, who at least seemed to take notice of Mustermann's existence. He approached him, hoe in hand and a little wobbly on his feet. Mustermann wondered about the man's disheveled appearance. It must have been a hard day's work, he concluded, because the gardener was also white as a sheet and his eyes looked sunken in his face. Mustermann noticed neither the gaping wound on the gardener's neck nor the madness in the man's eyes, who was assessing him, obviously setting on him as his next victim. Mustermann just wanted to be nice. He smiled, holding out his hand for a shake. The gardener dropped his hoe and slowly lifted his hat, as if to salute him. An oddly bulbous protrusion on his forehead came into view. Writhing and pumping, a dark mass was twitching behind almost translucent skin. The overall impression was definitely off-putting. Mustermann let his hand sink. His case tumbled from his suddenly limp fingers onto the gravel. The gardener's eyes rolled back in his head. He grabbed Mustermann by the shoulders, sinking his teeth into the Undersecretary's neck. Locked in the gardener's vise-like grip, Mustermann dropped to the ground like a felled tree.

3.

Two hours earlier
Kreuzberg, elevated track of the subway line U1

Frank had been a student of biology at the Freie Universität Berlin for two semesters now. As he lived in Friedrichshain, he always took the U1 from its final stop at Warschauer Strasse across River Spree and from there all the way through Kreuzberg. Before it reached the triangular junction, the U1 moved along on an elevated track, supported by columns of steel, that ran between the buildings at third-floor level. "Gründerzeit"-style apartment houses, modern concrete blocks, and the occasional place of worship zoomed past the window without leaving Frank with a lasting impression. Eyes half closed and still fighting stupor after last night's party, he was slumped on a bench in the first car. He was dressed all in black and, with his hoodie and worn-out Doc Martens, liked to imagine himself as something of an urban rebel. An outcast who always sat in the last row on the bus, keeping his distance to the rest of humanity, watching and ever ready to deliver a cynical barb when the mood hit him. Frank had no idea what to do with his life. For reasons even unknown to himself, he had enrolled in biology a year ago, a decision he since regretted. Sadly, he wasn't of the stuff geniuses were made of. Yes, he had rated with an IQ of 167, but it had just been an online test conducted by himself, and he had needed two attempts to make the score. To hell with it, he thought. He took a pack of Aspirins from his pocket, squeezed a pill out of the blister foil, chewed, and dry-swallowed. Antithrombin deficiency. Thick blood, was the popular name of this condition, with the unfortunate tendency to coagulate. A genetic defect, which meant that he needed three pills of this blood thinner a day to prevent thrombosis.

The pill's aftertaste lingering in his mouth, Frank let his eyes roam. At this time of the day, it was a little after eleven a.m., the train wasn't very full. Most commuters were already at their jobs, which meant that he had to share the ancient narrow-gauge car with only three other people: a muscular working-class hero wearing blue coveralls, a natty Turkish guy, and a female student. The fact that they all seemed to be in their early twenties was the only thing they had in common. The woman Frank had already met. Her name was Sophia, a fellow student in the same year and an activist in the university's student association. Last semester's blue bag, sporting a huge pin with the legend "Refugees Welcome", had meanwhile been replaced by a satchel made of some kind of green and white checkered material with a tatty fringe. "Go Vegan!" its legend declared. Every semester seemed to call for its own slogan, Frank thought. A Che-Guevara pin and a sew-on rainbow flag completed the left-wing uniform. For Frank she was Political Correctness personified, spouting slogans and phrases without ever having aspired to a view of her own. One of those people who claimed that gender and ethnic background didn't make a difference, which, however, didn't stop them from constantly sectional-izing and evaluating the world according to categories only known to them. Activists like her, he thought, were the grave-diggers of critical discourse, always coming up with new taboos and insisting that certain things had better be left unsaid. Dogmatists, who were just full of themselves, and cookie-cutter anarchists, as far as Frank was concerned. They dealt with language in an Orwellian fashion, with the result that discrimination continued to take place in people's minds, but could not be called by its name any longer.

Frank gave Sophia the stink eye. Their aversion was mutual. When entering the train at Schlesisches Tor, Sophia had recognized him at once, veered away, and had hurried to the other end of the car. While he was an outcast, Frank mused, Sophia was definitely the cheerleading-type. The epitome of the quarterback's blonde girlfriend, albeit, with her dreadlocks and her artfully distressed jeans, a tree-hugging German version.

The sturdy stubble-headed workman groaned and started waving his hand-held gaming console from left to right. He must have slammed his formula-one bolide into some concrete pillar, Frank thought. This six-three, three-hundred-pounds behemoth to him was nothing but ignorance and feeble-mindedness come alive. Millions of years of evolution, come to a screeching halt. Darwin must have gotten it wrong somehow, Frank decided. *Survival of the fittest*, what a joke! This tub of lard probably found fulfillment in pickling his last ounces of brains in beer, when he wasn't busy jerking off in some port-a-john. The world was going to the dogs anyhow, for Frank there was no doubt about it. Because, hey, who was up to the job of saving it? The Turkish guy at the door maybe, who seemed to be fascinated studying his perfectly manicured nails? He looked like someone who worked as a coiffeur in the hip neighborhood of Prenzlauer Berg, giggling and blowing air-kisses to his gay friends, while he fooled around with the hair of some silly broad.

The train had been sitting at the platform of Hallesches Tor for over five minutes now. Sophia stood and impatiently walked to the front exit. When she pressed the button, the doors wouldn't budge.

"Any idea what's going on here?" Sophie addressed the Turkish guy.

"Probably a blown signal, like," he replied, the picture of ennui. "It won't be long."

"You have a signal?" She pointed to her phone.

The Turk swiped long tresses of hair off his face and took out his smartphone. "No," he said, studying the screen once more to make sure. "No bars. Nothing."

"Weird. I never had any problems around here."

"It'll be back soon," the Turk assured her.

"Hello?" Sophia waved her hand in front of the workman's face to attract his attention.

The man removed his ear pods. "What?" he drawled. To Frank it sounded like a question the guy frequently had to ask.

"Do you have reception?" Sophia insisted.

"Reception?"

"A signal. Can you make calls?"

"This is a PSP."

"What?"

"A PSP, like, you can't make calls with it." He lifted the hand-held gaming console.

"It's only good for gaming?"

"Yeah."

"Everything'll be okay again soon," the Turk said.

"Ahem," Frank interjected. "I can't quite share your optimism."

When the three looked in Frank's direction, he pointed at the platform, where the driver could be seen staggering along the benches in the waiting area as if on auto-pilot. He stopped, staring at the four like a man possessed. Next, he threw himself at the car, hammering against the doors until the panes began to shudder. Sophia jumped back with a scream. The driver continued to batter the glass with his fists. After a while he took off his hat and started to rub is oddly bulging forehead against the glass. Frank stood and took position closer to the window in order to get a better look at the driver. The bones supporting the man's forehead seemed to have liquefied. His skin was thin and translucent. Lymphatic fluid was oozing from an opening above his nose. It also looked as if something was moving behind the papery bubble of skin. Something that clearly didn't belong there. Frank stepped up closer to the pane. The mass consisted of worm-like creatures, writhing among porous brain-matter. When the driver's hammering against the window intensified, even Frank shrunk back.

"Oh, my God, the poor man," Sophia whispered, biting her lip.

The driver's eyes rolled back in his head. He turned and began staggering down the platform, until he was out of sight.

Frank turned around to the others. "What sick shit was this?"

"Police," Sophia mumbled to herself. "We have to call the police... and an ambulance."

"I'd rather suggest an exorcist," Frank scoffed.

"Can't you keep your stupid mouth shut for once?"

"Easy does it," the Turk soothed, glancing at his phone. "Still no reception."

The workman stuffed his console into a side pocket of his coveralls and raised his head. "I'm Kai."

"Good for you," Frank said derisively, massaging his temples with circular motions.

"I'm on my way to work." Kai was unperturbed.

"I guess you better forget about work," Frank shot back. "They'll need to get someone else to stack their beer-crates today."

"What?"

"Oh, don't listen to him." Sophie shook her head. "He's just being Frank, an idiot I know from school. I'm Sophia, by the way."

"Hi, Sophia."

"What are we going to do now, Kai?"

"No idea. What was wrong with this guy?"

"What do you think?" Frank retorted. "His brain's shot. There are tens of thousands like him in Berlin."

"Does he always act like this?" the Turk wanted to know.

"Oh, well, his bark is worse than his bite," Sophia replied.

"I'm Can."

"Is there an emergency button, Can?"

"Right at the door. But the sign says that it will only alert the driver."

Frank laughed. "For real? Praised be our safety system. They thought about everything."

"Where might the driver have gone?" Sophia asked.

Can shook his head. "No idea."

"I need to get out of here!" Frank announced. He opened a hatch above the door and pulled the emergency lever to release the doors.

"Don't do anything stupid," Sophia protested.

Frank ignored her. He shoved open the door and peered out onto the platform. There was no one in sight. Frank got out and walked up to the third car, where he took a peek through the open door. The driver sat on his haunches on the floor next to an unconscious woman, who had a bleeding neck wound. A black worm-like mass was bulging out his forehead, slowly slithered back and retreated into its translucent sack of skin. The driver looked up, staring at Frank with blank eyes. Next, he jumped up, limbs twitching, took a leap at Frank, and dragged him to the ground with him. Frank fought for his life, trying to push him away. But, like a rabid dog, the man kept on snapping at his neck, mouth open wide and teeth bared. His bulbous forehead pulsed, the worms performing an ecstatic dance among the softened brain-matter. Frank screamed. The man's teeth already were grazing his skin, when suddenly someone grabbed hold of him from behind, picked him up, and tossed him onto the tracks between two cars. Kai had rushed to Frank's aid. "Let's split," he said, strangely calm, and touched his back as if in pain.

"The stairs!" Sophia yelled in the background.

Led by Sophia and Can, the four raced down the steps und toward the station's exit. Next to the plane trees that lined Gitschiner Strasse, they came to a stop. A car sped past them. When it reached the corner of Mehringdamm, it plunged into a pedestrian without even slowing down. The man was catapulted into the air like a doll, slamming headlong into the tarmac. The driver just continued on, leaving his victim, arms and legs twisted, behind on the bloodied ground.

From the other end of the street rumbling sounds could be heard. It was a strange groaning and moaning that seemed to be coming from a thousand voices. The four spun around.

"What sick joke is this?" Frank said when he saw the figures approaching them. A phalanx of black-haired men with long beards was marching straight at them, taking up the entire street and sidewalk. The men wore golden chains around their necks; green bandanas inscribed with Arab lettering covered their foreheads. They gave the general impression of lowlife-cum-Islamist-warriors. Slowly and relentlessly like a second-wave tsunami, they moved on in tight formation. An Armageddon of convulsing bodies, a cacophony of harsh grunts. The four just stood there, rooted to the spot and unable to take their eyes off the spectacle. It was as if they were just bystanders instead of coveted objects of desire, the lusted-after prey of this frenzied mob.

"Holy shit!" Frank breathed, when there were only about one hundred yards between them and the marchers. A young woman, totally lost in the task of shooting selfies of herself and the crazed masses, was soon surrounded and dragged to the ground and vanished amid a sea of beards and bandanas.

"We… need… to get… away! Come on!" Can stammered, turned, and began to run.

Sophia and Frank exchanged open-mouthed stares.

"We need to follow him, fast," Kai urged, shaking Frank by the shoulder. He nodded, slowly and like in a daze, still unable to believe his eyes. For a moment he kept on standing there, thunderstruck and incapable to get his head around the fact that life as he knew it had obviously stopped existing.

4.

The Chancellor was happily fondling his brand-new privates, as recommended by his doctor in order to improve blood-flow, when Neumeier, his Chief of Staff, came bursting into the room without knocking. The Chancellor looked up annoyed, wondering whether it was worth the trouble to reprimand the man for this act of insolence. Subordinates were expected to be respectful. He was Chancellor of the Federal Republic of Germany, after all, and right in the middle of a highly successful first term in office. Not counting, of course, the three terms he had already served the country as a woman, before transitioning. He had proven to be quite flexible already while still in a female body, owing to his legendary ability to adapt. Now, after twelve years of female rule, polls had hinted that voters wanted a man as head of state again. Someone more territorial than the Chancellor had deemed it necessary for a woman to be. The Chancellor gazed at the photograph on his desk. Despite all efforts he had failed to persuade his husband to agree to a reverse transition, which now made them a same-sex couple. He took the picture, pulled open the top drawer of his desk, put the frame inside, and closed the drawer again. At least he could count on the support of the Queer interest groups now, he thought.

"*Ma'am...* er... *Mr...* Chancellor," Neumeier blurted out, gasping for breath and his face deathly pale. "Worrying reports have come in... so many... many..."

"Pull yourself together, Neumeier. Stop stammering."

"I... I... we aren't safe here any longer."

"What?"

"In Kreuzberg…" Neumeier staggered over to the desk and supported himself on the desktop, as if he had trouble staying on his feet. "People are attacking each other… tumultuous scenes and killings… mass murders. We never had something like this before. A police station has been raided."

"What? Social unrest? Here? In my country?"

"In Kreuzberg."

"Kreuzberg?"

"The whole thing started in the area of Hallesches Tor, around the headquarters of the Social Democratic Party."

"The Lefties? What do they have to do with it?"

"Actually, I don't think that they have anything to do with it at all."

"Why do they make such a big thing about nothing? I simply needed a new coalition partner, that's all there's to it. Those spineless tree-huggers just came in handy."

"I don't think that the killings… this is totally new… it… it got out of control."

"What's this nonsense, Neumeier?" The Chancellor rose, his hand wandering to his crotch. "Call my limo. I'll go over to the Reichstag straight away. Come on, move it."

"But… the session… it can't… it will have to be cancelled. Berlin isn't safe any longer."

"My dear Neumeier, I won't have some crazy Lefties stop me from speaking in Parliament."

5.

Kreuzberg, Mehringplatz.

Crazed with panic, people ran this way and that like a herd of cattle in a stampede. Can, Sophia, und Frank hurried into the entrance of the apartment complex. Frank held the door for Kai, who hadn't been able to keep up with them. Hands pressed to his belly, as if trying to hold it in, he constantly looked over his shoulder at the bearded men, who were in hot pursuit.

"Come on, man! You wanna get yourself killed, or what?" Frank hollered.

"No, I don't!" Kai called out, as if Frank had asked him a real question.

"Then move your ass!"

After Kai had reached the safety of the stairwell, Frank slammed the door behind him and leaned his whole weight against it. Their pursuers threw themselves at the glass. Heads met the pane with a crack. Soon, the first bulging bubbles burst, and a mass of worms, brain-matter squirted against the glass. The lock disengaged and the door started to give way.

"Help me, goddammit!" Frank screamed.

Now, also Kai pushed his heavy bulk against the door. Sophia, who had already run up a flight of stairs, returned and also clung on for dear life.

"Where's this Turkish guy?" Frank asked.

"Can's ringing all the doorbells," Sophia ground out, fighting for breath. "Nobody's answering so far."

"Go and check out what he's doing. We won't be able to hold them back much longer," Frank ordered.

Sophia let go of the door with a nod and shot up the stairs.

"Go and follow her," Frank said to Kai.

Kai shook his head, no. "I'm not gonna leave you alone."

"I'm fast. I'll be right after you. So, move it."

"You sure?" Kai asked.

"Just go, fat slob!"

Kai released the door and started dragging himself up the stairs, breathing heavily and holding on the railing.

Frank wasn't able to keep the door from being slowly pushed open, until a bearded head squeezed itself through the gap.

"We're right on top, fourth floor!" Sophie's voice echoed down the stairwell. "Come on up!"

Frank let go of the door at once and made a dash up the stairs. When the metal door was slammed into the concrete wall, the glass pane shattered. The number of figures rushing into the building was so large that they caused a bottleneck-situation obstructing their own progress. Trampling over the bodies of their brethren stuck in the doorway, the attackers began flooding the stairwell.

When Frank looked down the flights of stairs he saw one wave of bearded figures after the other streaming into the building and washing up the stairs like an unleashed relentless flash flood.

Sophia awaited him at the open door of a fourth-floor apartment.

"Barricade the door!" Frank yelled, slammed it, and secured it with the chain. "We need something to use for a barrier."

"The shoe cabinet over there," Sophia suggested.

"Hell, yes. Hurry!"

With Kai's help they picked up the cabinet, carried it to the door, put it down, and pushed it up to the threshold.

Frank turned to the others. "Whose place is this, by the way?"

"No idea," Sophia replied. "The door was open. Nobody home."

"Can we lock the door?"

Sophia shook her head, no.

"Maybe the poor guy just went to take down the garbage," Frank mused.

"Wrong time, wrong place," Kai responded.

Frank nodded. "You're damn right," he agreed. When he crossed the hall he discovered Can on the loggia, where he had taken cover behind a paper plant.

"Fucking coward!" Frank growled. He stepped out on the balcony, shoving Can from behind.

"Hush!" Can hissed, without turning around.

"What?"

"Just look at this."

Frank looked down on Mehringplatz, where bearded figures fell on people, dragging them down to sink their fangs into their necks. Crazed with rage, they rushed old men, attacked women, and didn't even spare children, all the while grunting like mindless beasts of prey, whose bloodthirst can never be satisfied. In their frenzied greed they just overran their victims, no matter if they tried to take flight or just resigned to fate and remained sitting on the benches around the square in a dazed stupor. Those who desperately tried to climb the column that rose from the fountain in the middle of the square were pulled down and slaughtered one after the other. Due its circular layout, the apartment complex surrounded the square on all sides, giving Frank on his fourth-floor-perch a view like in the tiers of a colosseum. From his box seat he had a good view of the futile attempts at self-defense, when those on the ground fought back kicking and screaming until they could fight no more and were grabbed by the bearded fiends. After the last scream had petered out, only grunting and slurping could be heard.

"Are these vampires, or what?" Sophia was the first to voice the thought that had also occurred to Frank and Kai.

"No," Can protested. "No way. Just look what's happening over there." He pointed at a woman, prone on the rim of the fountain. The bearded attacker, who had just bitten her neck, now bent over her, took off his green bandana, and started to rub his forehead against her wound.

"What is he doing?" Frank wondered aloud.

"She's being… sort of… like, fertilized," suggested Kai with an involuntary grin.

"You're so gross!" Sophie was outraged.

Frank frowned. "He might be right. It really looks as if he wanted to inoculate her with something."

"Inoculate?"

"To introduce something into her wound, I mean."

Sophie clamped her hand to her mouth, emitting gagging sounds. "You're so disgusting, the two of you."

"What are you blaming us for? They're the ones doing it," Frank tried to defend himself.

"Who are these guys?" Can asked, still curiously observing the attackers. Meanwhile, hundreds of them had removed their bandanas, rubbing themselves against the necks of their paralyzed victims. "Zombies?"

"These aren't Zombies, no way," Kai protested.

"How would you know?" Can said.

"I'm always doing Zombie games, like, on my PSP. They walk with their arms all stretched out making *oooh, oooh* or sometimes *uurg*. These guys are different somehow, you know? No way, that they're Zombies."

"Does it really make a difference what exactly they're called?" Sophia interjected.

"The bulge is also atypical," Frank continued sagely, like conducting a scientific debate.

"And they're not pale but have a suntan. These guys look like they're using sun lamps," Kai remarked. "The living dead don't like the sun."

"I won't be going down to check their vitals, that much is clear," Can said.

"With an infrared camera we could find out if they still have a body temperature," Frank suggested.

"Yeah, such a camera would be real cool to have." Kai grinned.

"Boys and technology," Sophia scoffed.

"Zombies like to eat brains, right?" Can asked.

"Not necessarily," Kai answered. "Some of them are also into, sort of, pulling the tubing out of people."

"Hmm, that's right."

"Maybe they're a crossbreed of zombie and vampire?" Can ventured.

Frank shot him a scathing look. "And how do you explain the beards and the green bandanas with the Arabic writing?"

"What about them?"

"Don't they ring a bell?"

"What bell is there to ring?"

"These are your brethren in faith, asshole. Your Salafist friends from the intercultural neighborhood centers in this city," Frank accused.

"Just stop it," Can sighed.

"Mind you, your friends seem to have rather rigid ideas when it comes to religion," Frank continued to needle him. "Just look. They didn't even spare your garden-variety hijab girls."

"The ladies in diving bells also didn't stand a chance," Kai added.

"They're called chadors," Can exasperatedly pointed out.

"The black widows with the slits for eyes have also bought it," Frank observed.

"These guys look like they're from the storm troops in the Icy Desert of Hoth in *Star Wars*. Just that they're wearing, like, black stuff," Kai stated. "They're Mombies," was his solution to the name problem.

"Mombies?" Frank repeated.

"Yeah. Half Muslim, half Zombie."

Frank smiled. "You're a real comedian, right?"

"That's what my dad always says," Kai proudly confirmed.

Can shook his head. "You're nuts, both of you."

"Half *person*, half Zombie," Sophia corrected, putting the emphasis on person.

"Resolutely PC, even in the face of the apocalypse." Frank shook his head.

"So? What's wrong with it?" Sophia shot back.

Frank was looking down on Mehringplatz, his face a mask of confusion. "The walking tents, the women wearing burkas that is, aren't being attacked," he stated surprised.

"No. The ladies're sort of hanging out in the corner over there." Kai had noticed the burka-wearers in a throughway of the apartment complex.

"Islamism, taken to the highest level," Frank challenged Can. "Your friends don't seem to be happy with anything less but full body veil."

"My *friends*?"

"Your brethren in faith, to be exact."

"Why don't you just get lost?" Can hissed, returning to the living room.

Frank pulled his phone from the pocket of his jacket and switched it on to check the display. "Any reception?" he asked Sophia, who shook her head, no.

"No internet, no phone. Now, I can't even post a pic under the hashtag #ZombieApocalypse. I shudder to think how many likes that might cost me. The end is near." Frank grinned.

"You're a comedian, too," Kai observed.

"Much worse than that."

"Much worse?"

Frank patted Kai's shoulder. "Never mind." The three left the balcony, Frank closing the door behind them.

"What we need is a shotgun," Kai declared. "Then, we'd be able to blow these guys' heads off."

"Great idea," Frank agreed. "The only problem being that we're not in the States. We're in good old Germany, meaning that an old-school hand-to-hand approach is called for if you want to survive this fucking Zombie Apocalypse. Say thanks to our laws on gun control." Frank turned to Can. "Whose place is this, by the way? The renter doesn't happen to be a Muslim, does he? Otherwise we could have tried to scare these buggers off by waving a Quran in their faces." Frank raised his upturned hands as if holding out a book in self-defense. "Behold, o ye Mombies, we're your brethren in spirit," he intoned in a singsong voice.

"Brethren…," Kai repeated with a laugh.

Can just wordlessly shook his head and walked out of the living room.

"Why can't you just leave him alone?" Sophia chided.

"Leave him alone? We've left his lot alone for much too long. That's exactly why we're stuck in this clusterfuck now."

"Stop discriminating against him."

"Discriminating," Frank groaned. "Just the word I've been waiting for. Anything else you'd like to accuse me of? Racism maybe? Sexism? Just help yourself. But would you first please do me the favor to take a look out of the window? What is it again you guys keep on preaching? *We've overcome the concept of nation?* Hell, it makes me feel real glad that we're all perfect little Europeans now. Hey, citizens of the world even. Cardboard cutouts and a bit soft in the brain, but so what?" Frank started waving his arms in the air. "All differences, eradicated at last.

You people have finally got what you've wanted all along: You've turned us into a bleating flock of sheep."

Sophia started to open her mouth to give Frank a piece of her mind, when Can suddenly called out. They all went into the bedroom, where Can stood in front of the wall, admiring the skull-shaped masks hanging there. The room was entirely painted in black, the bed being made up with black sheets.

"What kind of place is this? Something out of *Pulp Fiction* or what?" Frank exclaimed.

"The guy might be a Goth," Sophia ventured.

"Goth?" Kai repeated.

Meanwhile Sophia had opened the closet. "No, a Goth he's not," she said, pointing at the whips and handcuffs dangling from hooks. "The gentleman rather seems to be into SM."

"SM?" Frank scoffed, casting a look at Can. "That's why you picked this place. Wherever our hearts lead us…"

"Won't you just leave him alone?" Sophia came to Can's defense. "Any suggestions on what we're supposed to do now?"

"Ask the Turkishman, he's the expert."

"Asshole," Can hissed.

Frank slammed out of the bedroom and marched down the hall back to the front door, where he supported himself on the shoe cabinet to peer through the peephole. "Fuck… they're still here!" he called, retracing his steps to the bedroom. "This shit we have your people to thank for. Fucking fanatics!" he hissed at Can.

"Just hold it," Sophia tried to calm him.

"What's your problem? These guys are his brethren in faith."

"They might as well be Christians."

"Just that they aren't."

"But they could be."

"And this discussion is helpful, because?"

"They are human beings."

Frank rolled his eyes. "Maybe before the worm got them. But not any longer." He strode up to Can and kept on shoving him, until he landed on the bed. "You never get enough, do you? Enjoying the freedom in our country and not being able to cope with it. Forcing your little girls to wear veils. Who do you think you are?"

Being of slight stature, Can new that he needed to avoid getting physical with Frank, who towered over him. He studied the floor.

Sophia stepped in, planting herself between Frank and Can. "Do you honestly think that this has something to do with Islam?"

"Oh, God, how I love this platitude! Does Islam have to do anything with anything at all? What *does* Islam have anything to do with? Not with religion, this much is clear. And definitely not with sanity."

"It's still better than your half-assed religion," Can blurted.

"Hear, hear, he's getting cheeky now."

"You're the ones who started the crusades. You've slaughtered the people of Jerusalem like cattle."

Frank huffed a mirthless laugh. "You seem to have forgotten, how your brain-numbing ideology has first spread to begin with. Fire and sword? Just to quote another catchphrase. This was a long time before the crusades, darling."

"We've brought civilization to barbarians like you."

"You've chopped off heads. Just like you do today. A gang of murderers, all throughout history and up to the present day."

"You're the ones who've helped ISIS to gain power," Can fought back. "You've started the wars in Afghanistan and Iraq."

"*We?* You're talking about the Yankees, right?"

"They're Christians, just like you are."

Frank smiled. "You can't be meaning me. Yes, I'm a Christian, but I don't practice any religion."

"Exactly that's your problem. You Germans so love to avoid commitment."

"Looking for trouble, Turk?" Frank's body language was definitely threatening.

Kai intervened. "Just stop arguing, both of you."

Sophia nodded in agreement. "Remember? Zombies? Out there?"

Frank glanced at his phone. Still no signal.

Can rose, walked over to the closet, and took out a black sheet which he carried through to the kitchen. When he returned he had pulled the fabric over his head. Two holes had been cut for the eyes.

"Time for a fancy-dress party?" Frank shook his head.

Can held a pair of scissors out to Sophia. "We don't want to give ourselves away. It worked for the veiled women, right?"

"You think we can fool them?" Sophia asked, took the scissors and pulled another sheet from the closet.

"Are you guys planning to do some kind of voodoo magic? We're scientists," Frank felt the need to remind Sophia.

"This is fun, like on Halloween," Kai enthused, grabbing the sheet with eye holes, Sophia had prepared for him, and dragged it over his head.

"I won't walk around in ghost costume, throwing myself at the mercy of Islamists. I'm going to get myself armed."

"There wasn't another sheet left in the closet anyway," Can laconically started.

"Shang's our Juggler," Kai announced.

"What are you talking about?"

"In computer games everybody has to be some character, like. And you're the Juggler."

Can smiled. "Maybe you're right."

When Frank returned with a mop, Kai, Sophia, and Can, all shrouded in black, had taken position in front of the bed. Frank had used packaging tape to attach a kitchen knife to the mop's handle, turning it into an improvised spear.

"Holy cow, what a gang of morons you are," was his comment on his companions' appearance. "Is this how you plan to scare off our bearded friends?"

Sophie held out the scissors. "You need to use the sheet from the bed. There isn't another one left."

Frank took the scissors, pointing them at the bed. "Do you seriously expect me to wear this dirty rag?"

"You've got no choice."

Frank pretended to take jabs at someone with his makeshift weapon. "No way. I'll give these bastards something to write home about."

"Where are we going to go from here?" Sophia asked.

"Just out of Kreuzberg, the rest we worry about later," Frank replied.

Sophia nodded. "Up Friedrichstrasse. I think we can make it to Checkpoint Charlie."

"We could use the subway tunnel," Can suggested.

"The U6 line?" Sophia asked.

Can nodded, yes. "I don't think there'll be still trains running. And the Zombies probably haven't yet made it down there."

"Let's check out the lay of the land," Sophia suggested. The four went out to the loggia, looking down on the square below them.

"What the hell is this?" Can didn't trust his eyes. Transfixed, the four stared down on the bearded men who had started to march around the pillar crowned with a copper angel that rose from the middle of the square.

"That's even crazier than I've feared," Frank exclaimed. "What do you make of this? Jaw-dropping, ain't it?"

"I… I… am," Can stammered.

"It looks like they've switched into pilgrimage-mode," Frank declared, the voice of authority. "Now they're doing their Mekka-thing."

Sophia touched Can's shoulder. "Don't worry about him. I know it has nothing to do with your religion," she assured him.

"We're not like this," Can insisted, still staring at the mob. "We're kind people. We're not some freaked-out…"

"You're worm-infested fanatics. That's what you are. It's part of your nature," Frank shot back, pointing his finger at the Zombies.

From the hall there was a clicking noise, as if someone had inserted a key into the look of the front door.

"What the hell…? What's going on?" Frank asked, confused. "Can these creatures also open doors?" Brandishing his mop-cum-spear, he raced to the front door, where a crack was slowly appearing. The cabinet was being pushed back, and the chain began to tighten. A head came into view. "What's happening here?" a bald-headed middle-aged man asked. "What are you doing in my place?" Next, they could hear him scream. "Oh, my God!" A hand came down on the man's head, yanking him away from the door. Kai and Sophia came running. They unhinged the chain and dragged the cabinet out of the way. Frank opened the door all the way. He raised his spear and rammed it into the forehead of one of the Zombies, who had thrown themselves on the owner of the apartment. When the knife got stuck in the bearded creature's skull, it was torn free of the mop's handle. Meanwhile, two more Zombies had overpowered the screeching tenant and taken him down. Their comrades turned their attention to Frank who tried to withdraw into the apartment. But no matter how hard he hurled his weight against the door, the Zombies outnumbered him and forced their way in. Like an unleashed flood, they filled the hall and lumbered after Frank, while ignoring Kai, Sophia, and Can

37

in their disguise. Frank barely managed to slam shut the bedroom door, before the Zombies had a chance to grab him.

The hammering against the door soon became deafening. First one fist, then two, then three, were working the wood. The door creaked and shuddered in its hinges. Frank desperately looked around the room. The window was too small for an escape route. He opened the closet, took out a pair of handcuffs, and put them in his pocket. No weapon in sight. He looked over to the door. No key in the lock. He grabbed the stained sheet off the bed, tore two holes for his eyes, and pulled it over his head. Then, he just stood staring at the door handle. "Bugger," he mumbled. The thumping against the door increased in volume. Next, the handle was pushed down and two Zombies lurched into the room, bodies convulsing, mouths open wide, and foreheads bulging. The color of the worms writhing behind translucent skin kept on alternating from red to green. The Zombies' orbs had sunk deep into their skulls, as if sucked in by their shrinking brains. Their vacant eyes didn't seem to notice Frank who, motionless and unrecognizable under his black shroud, remained standing next to the bed. When he slowly approached the door, he was jostled but nobody tried to stop him. Keeping close to the wall, he tiptoed down the hall. The Zombies replaced their bandanas to push bulges plus worms back into their skulls. With no victims in sight, they seemed to fall into a stupor. Frank reached the stairwell and took the stairs down. There were only a few Zombies standing around in a daze, but he didn't see any people. Sophia, Ka, or Can seemed to have vanished into thin air. The entrance to the subway station "Hallesches Tor" was located right at the building's front door. Maybe the others had stuck to their plan and were now running along the tracks toward "Mitte". There was a long-haired blond man on the stairs leading down to the platform. Dressed in light-colored cotton and Birkenstocks. Type aging hippie. His face was ashen, his eyes had sunk back in his skull, a sweatband masked his bulbous forehead. He still held his roll up mat tucked under his arm. The days of yoga were definitely over for him, Frank thought. And he realized that this was the first but by no means the last convert he'd be coming across.

6.

In the Garden of Schloss Bellevue

Undersecretary Mustermann opened his eyes, peering into the brilliantly blue sky. Without thinking he touched his head, checking the state of his hairstyle. His comb-over had remained in place in spite of the fall. He continued to move his palm down his face. When he reached his throat, his hand got stuck on an obstacle. He plucked at it, but it wouldn't budge. A look down his body told him, that he was holding a flap of skin. When he let go of it, the skin snapped back into place. He fingered the deep wound on his throat, running his fingertips along exposed blood vessels. But there was no blood, and he also didn't feel any pain. He quickly sat up and looked around. The park was deserted, but on the street a parade seemed to be in progress. A crowd of thousands was pushing its way through Tiergarten in the direction of the Reichstag Building. Was it really a parade? What day was today? No matter how much Mustermann racked his brain, he simply couldn't remember. The happenings of this morning, however, were still vividly present in his mind. His wife had left him and had gone to live with her parents in Munich, taking their two children with her. A bed-wetter and a weakling, this was what she had called him. A spineless flunky, to boot. She had the nerve to leave him, even though she was the one with the affair! He remembered how he had stood there for a long while, silent and briefcase in hand, while she had announced her decision. He had just turned and walked out. At least he didn't have his children to worry about. According to their marriage contract she was entitled to eighty percent of his paycheck, after all. No reason to complain, as far as she was concerned. But the twenty percent left for him were more than enough. Also, today was to have been his day of limelight in the Office of the Federal President. A little ceremony had been planned to award him for his loyal services. However, it wasn't meant to be. His wife wasn't the only one who had abandoned him today. The Chancellor had left in his helicopter without once looking back. Mustermann rose, gazing across the lawn to the street, where people were goose-stepping by like in a trance, their movements oddly jerky. Like in a procession, they were marching to a monotonous tune of grunting and groaning. Mustermann wondered why there wasn't any music being played. Some modern cacophony like on the day he had set foot into a dance club the first and only time in his life. Even now, after all these years, Mustermann sometimes woke up in the middle in the night, tortured by flashbacks of this traumatic experience. The thudding basses still in his ears, his class-mates' convulsions on the dance floor still in front of his mind's eyes. Shameless and frenzied, they'd been making out, backlit by strobing lights. Mustermann involuntarily shook his head. There was nothing that scared him more than losing control like this. He preferred to keep in the background, like a butler always ready to serve. When a piercing pain shot through his skull, he squeezed his eyes shut and rubbed his forehead.

You're nothing but a measly minion, a voice from behind seemed to whisper into his ear.

When Mustermann turned, there was no one around.

You've always been just a spear-carrier in your own life, a thought tiptoed through his mind. Again, the piercing pain. Mustermann ran his hand across his forehead once more. He took off his suit jacket, let it drop to the ground, loosened his tie, and opened the top button of his shirt.

For the President you're no better than a piece of furniture. He's discarded you like a wobbly chair.

There was this voice again. Mustermann performed a full turn. There still was nobody to be seen. Who was this voice talking to him?

The President has betrayed you. He's taken off without you.

He must have had a good reason, Mustermann protested.

Yeah, right, sure he did. It's because you're absolutely useless.

Useless? I'm the President's most senior Undersecretary.

A pathetic brown-noser, that's what you are.

Am not.

Why don't you look straight ahead?

Mustermann complied, still rubbing his forehead.

What do you see?

People marching down the street.

They aren't people any longer.

But they look like people.

They still aren't. They've received The Bite.

Bite?

Do you know where they're heading?

No.

They're thirsting for revenge.

Revenge?

They demand payment from those who've betrayed all of you. Those, who've given you up. Those, who have closed their ears and taken abuse of the constitution.

I don't quite understand…

They need you.

Need me?

You have to be their leader.

Their leader?

To lead them on the right path.

I can't. I'm too weak.

You're a part of our community now. We'll provide you with the strength and the power you've always wished you had. We'll save you.

Who are you?
We're many.
What do you want?
We want to build a new society.

Again, there was a searing pain, filling Mustermann's skull. He continued rubbing his forehead. Over and over, until his palm started to feel warm. Still he went on rubbing, as if to scrub the pain away.

7.

On the tracks of subway line U6.

Hampered by darkness and the slits in his sheet, Frank could hardly see where he was going. Keeping to the ties between the tracks to orient himself, he felt his way down the subway tunnel. About half a mile separated him from the next station. From time to time he stopped and listened for the sounds of an approaching train or strange noises signaling the arrival of Zombies. Once there seemed to be footsteps on gravel somewhere in the distance but when he listened more closely, everything was quiet. There was no sign of either Sophia, Can, or Kai and he had no idea if they had even taken refuge in the subway system at all. Finally, he saw a light behind the next bend, probably coming from "Kochstrasse" station. A train was waiting there, ready to depart. Frank left the tracks and dashed up the stairs, leading to a maintenance platform, where he knelt to listen again. Silence. Frank pulled the sheet over his head, bundled it up, and draped it over his shoulders. He picked up a length of metal piping from the ground and tiptoed to the open door of a room, which seemed to serve as a breakfast-room for the track workers. He peered inside. A number of men wearing security vests had gathered around a table and were drinking beer. On the ground in front of them there were four dead bodies in a large pool of blood. Their foreheads had been smashed. Blood, worms, and brain-matter had formed a puddle on the concrete floor. Frank crept past the door and to an unlocked grate that opened unto the platform of "Kochstrasse" station. Behind the ticket booth, whose windows had been covered with mirrored foil since it went out of operation, he saw three figures scurrying along. Shrouded in sheets, they resembled Halloween ghosts. Kai, whose sheet only came down to his knees, noticed him first.

"Frank!" he called out happily, turning to the others. "See? I've always known that he'd make it."

Frank ignored him, rushing Can instead to give him a violent shove. "Why the sheets? How did you know?" he demanded.

Can pushed him away. "Are you crazy, man?"

"How did you know that the sheets would help?" Frank threatened, raising his metal pipe.

Sophia stepped between them. "What's wrong with you?"

"The Turkishman knows something. They're all working together, these guys. These fucking Muslim bastards."

"You've no idea what you're talking about," Can defended himself. "Islam means peace."

"Peace?" Frank sneered with a laugh. "Yeah? Whenever I hear Muslims talking peace, the movie *Mars Attacks* comes to mind. 'We bring you peace'," he intoned in a falsetto voice to imitate the Martians. His hand shaped like a gun, he fired imaginary shots at the others, making laser-canon noises.

"It's all a matter of interpretation," Can continued to stand up for his faith.

Frank waved him off. "Yeah, right. Everything's just in the eye of the beholder," he scoffed. "Some people even try to sell you a Zombie flick like *Dawn of the Dead* as an anti-consumerist statement. Meanwhile, the rest of the world just enjoys the gore and spatter. Doesn't Jihad also stand for something like *strenuous endeavor*? Well, if you think about it, chopping off heads must give you pretty good exercise."

"Just shut the fuck up, asshole," Can hissed. "Just in case you're interested, I'm Kurdish not Turkish."

"Same, same."

Can turned and walked a couple of steps. "You guys really have no clue!"

45

"Clue about what? You mean to say that you do know what's going on here?" Frank asked.

Can pivoted on his heels, yanking off his sheet. "I know shit. The only thing I do know is how to survive. Which is by not attracting attention. And if these ISIS douchebags can tolerate women only if they're wearing burkas, then that's what they'll get."

"What are you trying to say?"

"That I don't understand what's happening any better than you do. The only thing I know is that you have to go with the flow."

"You used the sheet, because the Zombies…"

"The Mombies," Kai corrected.

"Never mind," Frank continued. "Because these guys spared women wearing burkas?"

"I keep my eyes open and try to fit in."

"What are you talking about. Are you some kind of *Zelig* type, or what?"

"A what?"

"Well, like the guy from the movie. Woody Allen? You've probably never heard of him in Anatolia."

"I don't know *Zelig*, either," Sophie interjected. "Why don't you just explain it to us. Is it a film about mimicry or something like it? Like a grasshopper pretending to be a leaf?"

"Yeah, you could say so. The character Zelig is one of the people who blend in with the wallpaper," Frank replied. "He simply becomes the person others want him to be. He always does his best to adapt. When he talks to doctors, he only needs a few minutes to start speaking perfect medicalese. And he doesn't end it at that: He even changes his physical appearance and suddenly wears a white coat and such."

"How does he do it?"

"No idea. It doesn't need to be realistic. And when he talks to rabbis, he suddenly sports a long beard. He's someone who has internalized conformity to perfection, which even enables him to change shape. Therefore, it's impossible for him to have an opinion of his own. He totally blends in with his surroundings."

"I would have taken you for a Chuck Norris man," Sophia jibed.

"What?"

"Well, *Law and Order*. That's your thing, right? I would have never guessed that you're into Woody Allen."

"I still prefer Chuck to your friend Che, the murderous bastard," Frank retorted.

"You've no idea," Sophia protested.

"Of course I'm not as well informed as the brainy members of your student union coffee club."

"Whenever you run out of points to make you start insulting people."

"Points? I haven't heard anyone making points yet."

"My dad always went to the car racing track," Kai interrupted.

"What?"

"He always like watched the races. When the drivers step on the gas and pull the brakes at the same time, the wheels just start to spin. What an awesome noise. You can't hear anything else. The noise covers up all the chattering, my dad always said. Yes, that's what he said."

Frank nodded in respect. "A wise man, your dad." He walked to the edge of the platform, peered into the dark tunnel, turned, and came back to the others. "Let's go. Kai, you bring up the rear."

"Rear? Cool, like in Ego Shooter," was Kai's excited reaction.

"Why do you want to be up front?" Sophia asked.

"Why I want...? What? Because you need a formation. The strong ones on the outside and the weak ones in the middle. You're a biologist, right? Baboons also march in formation when they're threatened."

"Baboons? What cave did you crawl out of?"

"Sorry, missy, I just forgot that we're living in times of *Gender Uber Alles*. Okay, then I'd better switch off my survival instinct." Frank raised his hands in surrender. "So what? I've always been convinced anyhow that the two sexes are nothing but an invention of the Croatian betting mafia."

Kai laughed. "The mafia?"

"Just think about it," Frank continued, a mischievous grin on his face. "Due to the artificially imposed categories of male and female, which, as well all know, don't exist, we can have twice the number of competitions in all fields of sports. One for men and one for women. Twice the number of competitions means twice the amount of bets, which translates into double profit."

"That's the dumbest shit I've ever heard." Can shook his head.

"Well, I guess you've never witnessed a meeting of the student union," Frank replied. "Sophia, then you tell us what to do next. Now it's time to own up. No more discussions. Our situation calls for immediate action. No worrying about sensibilities, no balancing of opinions, but a hands-on approach."

"Gender studies are a recognized field of academic research, asshole."

"Of course they are. And our out-of-control bearded friends out there are the products of some Yankee conspiracy with the aim to discredit Islam."

"They don't look like Yankees to me," Kai stated, his tone matter-of-fact. He pointed toward the end of the platform, where three Zombies had noticed them and now started their approach. They looked like small-time thugs, dressed in the usual uniform of sweatpants. Slowly, they lumbered closer. Frank raised his iron bar and made ready to face them. When there were only a few yards left between him and his opponents, the Zombies removed their bandanas and presented their foreheads.

"You'd better watch out," Frank warned. "You're messing with the wrong person here. I'll teach you!" Frank drew back his iron bar and smashed it into the first Zombie's forehead. The skin burst open. Blood, worms, and brain-matter sloshed on the tiled platform floor. Frank rammed his bar into the forehead of the second Zombie. And when the third tried to take him into a strangle hold, he grabbed him by the throat with one hand and pummeled his face with his fists, until the Zombie collapsed. Frank swung his bar and continued battering the Zombie, who soon stopped twitching.

Kai, Can, and Sophia were wordlessly watching from a distance.

"Well, it wasn't a big thing, right?" Frank ground out, panting. "Your bearded friends don't seem to be the sharpest knives in the drawer, Can."

"Oh, great. The apocalypse hasn't even properly started yet, and he's already going nuts," Can commented.

"You've got something in your face," Kai said to Frank.

"What?"

"On your forehead."

When Frank moved his hand across his forehead, his fingers touched something slimy. He peeled it off and tossed it to the ground.

The four gathered around the gooey substance, writhing on the tiles.

"Is this really the stuff they have inside their heads?" Can asked.

"Looks like it," Sophia confirmed.

"That's an earthworm," Kai decided. "These guys aren't Mombies after all," he added, his voice filled with disappointment.

Sophia pulled the sheet off her head and bent down. "This thing can't be an earthworm. Earthworms are articulate animals, which means that their segments are all the same size. This beauty here is just an amorphous mass. More like some kind of leach."

Frank used a corner of his sheet to clean his face. "Shit... is it possible that I might be...?" Sheer horror was reflected in his eyes. "Will I turn into one of them now?"

"I don't think so," Sophia replied. "Just look at these guys." She pointed a finger at the dead Zombies. "They have wounds on their necks. This seems to be the thing that does the trick. The bite."

"You sure?" Frank was not convinced.

"Pretty sure."

A gust of wind hit them and a screeching sound announced the arrival of a train. The four turned around.

"We need to split," Frank whispered.

"Where to?" Sophia asked.

"Out of here. Up the stairs," Frank suggested.

They ran toward the exit, where they stopped when the train entered the station. The train came to a halt, however, with only the first two cars alongside the platform, while the rest remained inside the tunnel. The driver behind his console seemed to be semi-conscious. He was bobbing his head and fumbled for the right control on the panel. As soon as he'd found it, the doors opened and dozens of Zombies came rushing out. They were second-generation converts, their foreheads hidden under base caps, hard hats, and even t-shirts they had taken off to use them as headgear. Momentarily confused, one of the Zombies more or less accidentally looked in their direction. He issued a grunt, and soon the others, too, had discovered their prey. Kai, Can, Sophia, and Frank turned and dashed up the stairs of "Kochstrasse" station.

"Why don't you put your sheets back on?" Sophia chided Frank and Can.

"With this thing I can't see where I'm going!", Frank complained. "Maybe it's stopped working its magic anyhow."

"Checkpoint Charlie" was right in front of them. Without a care in the world, tourists had their photos taken with actors dressed up in American uniforms. Not even the grunting mob that now came storming up the stairs from the station was able to stop them from posing in front of a wall of sandbags.

"The shop over there!" Sophia called out, pointing at the One-Euro discount store across the street. They ran inside, closed the glass doors, and blocked them with two heavy display bins.

"What do you think you're doing?" the sales lady protested.

"Haven't you noticed what's happening out there?" Sophia shot back. "Zombies… the end of the world has come."

"Does apocalypse ring a bell?" Can added.

"I've no use for your stupid Halloween nonsense right now. Just put those bins back, move it," the lady hissed.

The screams of tourists brought down by Zombies could be heard inside the store.

"See?" Frank said, raising his metal bar.

"Are you making a movie or what?" The sales lady still didn't seem to grasp the gravity of the situation.

Can shook his head, no. "Don't you understand? There are Zombies out there!"

"I've had it. Of you and of your ridiculous Zombies, too. My son also doesn't do anything else but watch this bullshit."

A convert picked this moment to throw himself against the shop window. He lifted his base cap and started to rub his bulge against the glass.

The sales lady screamed. "Jesus, what are these creatures doing out there?"

"My dear ma'am," Can replied with a flourish, "allow me to introduce you to the living dead." The Zombie remained motionless, as if affixed to the pane with suction cups.

"Holy shit," the lady cursed. "We just had the window cleaners in today."

Frank walked to the door, brandishing his iron bar. After a moment of thought he turned to the sales lady. "Do you happen to have a Quran handy?"

"I…"

"A Bible wouldn't be bad either. As a point of reference, so to say."

"What are you up to?" Sophia asked.

"A little experiment on our clingy friend out there. Maybe it'll work."

The sales lady handed him a Quran and a Bible from under the counter.

"You're prepared for all events, right?" Frank said.

"One Euro buys you a lot of things," the lady replied.

Frank held the Bible right under the Zombie's sunken eyes. Trembling with excitement and not leaving Frank out of his sights, the Zombie began to hammer even more furiously against the pane.

"This was the negative control, I guess," Frank said, turning to the others. "And now let's see how he responds to this." Frank held out the Quran. But the Zombie's eyes still didn't leave his face. "Well, the Quran doesn't seem to do the trick either."

"Just give the fucker a phonebook to chew on," Kai suggested.

Frank smiled. "Maybe you're right."

"I've an idea what the problem might be," Sophia said.

"Speak up," Frank replied.

"If I'm not mistaken…" Sophia began.

"Rita?" the sales lady interrupted. "What are you doing here? It's your day off."

The woman she had addressed approached them from the back of the store, bumping into display bins on her way. She wore a pair of panty hose wrapped around her forehead, and, judging by her vacant eyes, she didn't seem to enjoy being off from work.

Frank stepped up to her, brandishing his metal bar. But the sales lady blocked his way. "Don't you dare harm her, boy, or you'll have me to deal with."

"Listen. Don't you see that there's something wrong with Rita?"

The Zombie made a grab for her co-worker, trying to dig her fangs into her neck.

"Rita? What are you doing?" the shop lady complained. Kai leaped at the Zombie, closing his arms around her from behind. Like a snapping turtle attacking its prey, the Zombie continued to go for her co-worker's neck. But her struggles were in vain, as she was unable to extricate herself from Kai's vise-like grip.

When Frank raised his metal bar, the shop lady held on to his arm.

Please, please don't," she pleaded.

"What do you want us to do?" Frank replied. "I need to end her misery."

"No!"

"Let me give it a try," Can interjected. He took a roll of garbage bags, unrolled one bag, pulled it over the Zombie's head, and drew the strings tight. The Zombie's grunts ceased at once and she quieted down like a parrot when its cage is covered with a blanket.

"Shang has bagged Rita," Kai grinned.

"And now?" Frank asked. "Kai can't restrain her forever."

"Don't worry, I'm fine," Kai protested. "I'm just not allowed to lift heavy weights. Doctor's order."

"The staff toilet," the shop lady suggested. "Just lock Rita in there and give her a chance to recover."

"Recover?" Frank repeated, staring at her aghast. "Are you sure?"

"Why don't you just do it?" Sophia ordered.

Without effort, Kai dragged the Zombie to the staff toilet, where he deposited her on the toilet seat.

"She needs a hole to breathe, or she'll choke to death," Sophia said.

"Are you joking?" Frank answered. "That's the least of her problems right now, don't you think so?"

Sophia bent over the Zombie who was sitting like frozen on the toilet seat and tore open the bottom of the bag.

"Come on! Over here!" Can called nervously from the front of the store. Frank locked the door to the toilet behind him, and then they all hurried to the sales area. Meanwhile, dozens of bleating and grunting Zombies had gathered at the window, pressing their faces against the glass.

Frank shook his head. "They're stuck to the window like blowflies. We'll never get out this way."

"Is there a back door?" Can asked.

"Yes," the shop lady replied.

"I'll check out the route," Frank announced. "You all wait here." He turned to the shop lady. "Show me the way to the back yard."

The shop lady nodded, yes.

Can followed the other two through the store, where he stopped at a bin filled with box cutters. He took one and pocketed it after breaking open the packaging. "One Euro," he mumbled. "What do you expect for this price?"

Sophia had collected a roll of garbage bags, a bottle of water, and a screwdriver. She walked up to the counter and put three Euros next to the register. Kai was staring at the Zombies who were still glued the window. His eyes wandered over their heads to Checkpoint Charlie, where an American Zombie soldier, flag in hand, had sunk his fangs into an Asian tourist. In the first-floor café across the street people still sat, peacefully enjoying a piece of cake. Kai couldn't believe his eyes. He remembered something his father had often said about him: His processor might be a bit slow and his clock frequency a little dated, but time-tested computers turned out to be the most trustworthy sometimes. While he observed the smiling people in the café, shopping bags under their tables, he came to the conclusion that his father had been right all along.

"What do you see?" Sophia asked, approaching him from behind.

"That I'm not the dumbest idiot around here," Kai replied.

"Why do you say something like this? Of course you're not."

"Right. It's just that now I can be absolutely sure."

Can went to the cooler, took out a bottle of cola, and took a deep drink. When his lips enclosed the neck of the bottle, a bit of the brown liquid kept on sloshing back with a chugging sound.

"Don't forget to pay, young man," the shop lady said when she and Frank returned.

"For real?"

"There's no such thing as a free lunch," the shop lady replied.

"Aw, shit, we're having a Zombie Apocalypse and I'm still expected to pay? That's so totally uncool!"

"You've heard the lady. One Euro, I suppose," Frank addressed the woman.

"Like every item in this store," she confirmed.

Can dug the coin out of his pocket, pressing it into the shop lady's hand.

"I've found a way out," Frank announced.

"Ahem… there's something sticking to your iron bar…" Can ventured.

Frank gazed at the hairs that had fused with clotted blood and torn skin on the bar's surface. "We had an unwelcome guest," he said matter-of-factly. "We need to go to the second floor. There's a vacant apartment. From there we'll climb out the front window and onto the scaffolding. Then it's down to Kochstrasse and a dash along Wilhelmstrasse. Maybe we'll make it to the Reichstag Building."

"Why do you want to go there?" Can asked.

"There's bound to be police around," Frank replied reasonably.

"Ready," Kai called out, mimicking a salute.

"I'm not sure if that's the right route," Sophia voiced her doubts.

"We need to follow him, Sophia," Kai said. "Frank's the Scout."

"The Scout?"

"He leads the way."

"See, sweetie, he's on my side."

"Can, what do you think?" Sophia still wasn't convinced.

Can pulled the sheet over his head. "Well, staying here isn't an option."

"Okay," Sophia reluctantly agreed. "Let's go."

The four set out on the route Frank had discovered. No one else wanted to join them, neither the sales lady from the One-Euro discount store nor the scared people inside the apartments they passed on their way across the scaffolding.

"Why don't you put your sheet back on?" Sophia said to Frank while they were climbing down a ladder.

"I'm not hiding any longer," Frank declared.

"You'll endanger all of us."

"No way I'm gonna wear this wanked up rag again." Frank was adamant.

"What?"

"Your sheets are clean, remember? I had to use the one from the bed."

Sophia touched his shoulder. "But it's faces they respond to. That's why they left the burka ladies alone and let us pass at Mehringplatz."

"They're fucking Zombies. Maybe even Zombies from some type of Muslim training camp."

"You're a scientist, Frank," she implored him. "You know that this madness has nothing to do with Islam."

"Bullshit! They're all the same: worms and Islamists." Frank strode over to a souvenir vendor who was prone and lifeless on the ground. Bending down, he picked up a toy gas mask that, together with little flags and Red-Army style woolly hats, had been part of the man's stock. "If you're right," Frank said, putting on the gas mask. "Then this thing here ought to do the trick." He ran over to Friedrichstrasse and planted himself in the path of the approaching Zombies, both arms spread.

"What a nutcase!" Can murmured, incredulous.

Frank was soon engulfed by a mass of Zombies, who parted around him and just continued on their robot-like march, in the search of fresh prey. Frank remained standing there, unharmed and arms still spread, while the Zombies kept lumbering on. "It worked," he said, amazed, when he joined the others.

Sophia gave a knowing nod. "I told you so. They respond to people's faces. That's what attracts them. And that's how they identify their victims."

The deafening thud of bases, a high-pitched female voice singing in Arabic. A Beemer sped toward them. The open window showed an Arab man with an eighties-style haircut. Kai, Frank, and Sophia barely managed to avoid the car by leaping onto the sidewalk. Can, however, stayed rooted to the spot. When the Beemer smashed into him, he was thrown back and tossed onto the blacktop. Still under shock, he jumped up, yanking the sheet off his body. The Arab just plunged his car into the next wave of Zombies, rolling down Friedrichstrasse. Bodies were blown in all directions, hurled about like dolls, and squashed by churning wheels. The driver lost control over his car, slamming it into a lamp post. A group of Zombies immediately lurched forward and began to form a circle around the vehicle. The driver pulled a gun from the glove department and fired at three of his opponents, mowing them down, before running out of ammo. He slid over to the passenger seat and began kicking at the Zombies who tried to enter the car through the open window. When one of the Zombies noticed Can, now sans sheet, he turned away from the car, greedily staggering in his direction. Can, who was still in a daze, moved his hand over the cut on the back of his head. When he saw the blood on his fingers, he started to sway and collapsed on the ground. Frank grabbed him by both arms and dragged him off the street. His eyes were fixed on the Zombies who had meanwhile finished off their prey and were now abandoning the Arab's car to turn on them.

"We need to carry Can! Hurry!" Sophie yelled.

"Carry him I can, I'm just not supposed to lift him," Kai said.

"You're stronger than the rest of us," Frank agreed, hoisting Can on Kai's shoulders. "Run over to the memorial. I'll follow you," he added.

"Where to?" Sophia asked.

"Up on the steles of the memorial!" Frank called out and turned to face the Zombies, metal bar raised. "Come on, you fucking bastards. I'll show you," he roared.

Can across his shoulders, Kai ran after Sophia toward the steles of the Holocaust memorial, while Frank launched his attack at the Zombies. But as he was wearing his gas mask, they just ignored him. "Buggers," Frank whispered, hurrying after the others.

The steles of the memorial gradually increased in height the deeper you progressed into the heart of the oversized symbolic burial ground. Frank took a jump onto the first stele, which only came up to his knees. From there he vaulted onto the adjoining one, then to the one after, continuing on and on. The deluge of Zombies was parted by the narrowly spaced concrete blocks, where the creatures, unable to thread their way from stele to stele, got stuck in the canyons between the monoliths. Kai and Sophia had meanwhile taken refuge on top of a stele in the heart of the memorial that jutted up about 14 feet from the ground. Can was resting on his side, breathing hard and peering down on their attackers, who had gathered at their feet. They reached up to them, straining their necks and presenting their bulging foreheads.

8.

Inside the Reichstag Building, faction room of the Christian Democratic Party

The Chancellor and their chief of staff had retired to the faction room in the Reichstag Building's upper level to discuss the situation. The Chancellor's two security men guarded the door. Neumeier had opened his laptop to play a number of YouTube videos made by local citizens to his superior. The footage proved without a doubt that the city of Berlin now was a Zombie infested Armageddon. The Chancellor was still studying the shaky grainy pictures with interest, when suddenly the internet signal died.

"Unbelievable, the options we're having today, Neumeier. Holy smoke. Internet. It will be the thing of the future, I swear."

"I'm sure you're right," Neumeier agreed, while trying to hide his disbelief behind the façade of the ever jovial hedonist. "There're videos like this from almost all neighborhoods of Berlin," he explained.

"And what about the rest of the country?"

"The surveys are still in progress. We don't have the big picture yet."

"And the Reichstag?"

"Federal police have sealed all entrances. A number of platoons of Riot Police have been summoned to secure the building. However, only a handful of officers have reported for service. The members of Parliament have come together in the plenary hall. Emergency electricity supply will be available for another 72 hours."

"Is it really that bad?"

"According to the Federal Police we're dealing with some kind of plague, which makes people sprout worms from their heads."

"How annoying. But yes, I see your point. What about Parliament? The ability to function must remain our top priority. Give order to concentrate all available forces."

"What forces? There aren't any left. Riot Police seems to have disbanded."

"We'll need the Army, then."

"The Army and most Federal Police officers are engaged at the Bavarian border."

"They're at the border? All of them?"

"You've sent them there yourself before the last election. Don't you remember? The refugee crisis?"

"Which is now returned to us like a bloody boomerang. Hell! Okay, then we'll have no choice but to surrender Berlin. Just get me a flight out of here, Neumeier."

"Sorry, but we've run out of helicopters. We've also lost contact to Tegel Airport."

"What? No more helicopters?"

"You've cut the defense budget yourself last year, because the 'Grim Guardian of Revenues' insisted on zero government debt."

"Don't you ever mention this person again, Neumeier. Understood?"

"Yes, ma'am… sir…"

"In this case the Americans need to help us out."

"The Americans?"

"Yes, our transatlantic friends."

"They won't send any troops to Berlin, lest they aggravate the Russians even more."

"And the EU? Can't the EU step in?"

"In the light of this extremely critical situation it has been decided to schedule a special meeting next week."

"*Next week?*"

"However, the President of the EU Parliament assures you of his complete solidarity in the face of this difficult crisis. The President of the European Commission, too, is deeply concerned because of the number of casualties."

"What a bunch of douchebags!" the Chancellor cursed. "Okay. If this is the way it is, the emergency plan needs to be put in motion."

"Emergency plan?"

"The master plan. Like during the Cold War."

"In Eastern Germany they had something like this, not in the Federal Republic, though, because according to our scenario the entire country would have been wiped out by Soviet nuclear weapons anyway. Too bad that there has never been a change of strategy after the Wall came down."

"Damn. Isn't this what I've been talking about all along, Neumeier? We shouldn't have been so fast in doing away with everything East German."

"If you say so, Chancellor, ma'am... er... sir..."

"Let's retire to the bunker, then. We'll just need to lay low until somebody'll show up to save us. Duck and cover, that's the motto of the day."

"Well, I need... I..." Neumeier stammered. "Unfortunately... I can't think of the right way to put it. Berlin International Airport isn't the only failed government project, you know?"

"What are you talking about?"

"Three years ago the bunker construction site was flooded by River Spree, which resulted in serious damage. The ensuing cavity was later filled with sand to prevent the Reichstag's foundations from being destabilized. And now... well... there aren't any shelters down there. There isn't anything, actually. Just sand."

"No shelters?"

"No, ma'am… err… sir…"

Neumeier's laptop announced an incoming video call.

"What's that?" the Chancellor asked.

Neumeier glanced at the screen. "It's the President of the Republic."

"Deutsch?" the Chancellor replied. "Where the hell is he?"

"Just a moment." When Neumeier accepted the call, President Deutsch appeared on the screen, his arms resting on his desk. Behind him, an escort of soldiers, all clad in historic Prussian uniforms, was standing at attention.

"Deutsch? Where are you, goddammit?" the Chancellor demanded to know.

"I'm in Weimar," the President answered, his voice sounding almost reverently.

"*Weimar*?"

"Right. Where the first German Republic was proclaimed after World War One."

"Who are those people with you? And why are they wearing these silly uniforms?"

"They, Chancellor, are my personal bodyguards. In the light of our extremely critical situation, I kindly ask you to entrust me with ruling the country from my new seat of Government, here in Weimar."

"What? Ruling the country? Have you… gone mad?"

"I've feared that my request might fall on deaf ears. Sadly, you don't give me a choice. I see no other way out of our predicament, if we want to prevent our country from turning in to a dysfunctional state."

"Are you out of your mind, Deutsch?"

"I have to end our conversation now. I wish you well and God's blessing," Deutsch replied, crossing himself.

"I tell you what... Deutsch!" the Chancellor hollered, but the connection had ended. "Neumeier, did you hear what he just said?" The Chancellor was livid.

"It was impossible to miss, madam... err... sir. Our President seems to have changed his job description on a unilateral basis."

"Our constitution doesn't provide for something like this. The President's duties are of an exclusively representative nature. He's not my second-in-command."

"Herr Deutsch has a quite different view on this matter, I'm afraid."

"This guy is a joke!"

"The President plans to amend the constitution, I assume. With the support of the Church."

"The Church?"

"He's well connected."

The Chancellor's expression turned thunderous. "This disgusting, greedy..." He huffed a mirthless chuckle. "IM Maggot. This was his code name as an informal agent of the secret service, when Eastern Germany was under Communist rule. The goddamn fucker still seems to live up to his name."

"What?" Neumeier was confused.

„Might Deutsch have... The Stasi? The Eastern German secret service? He might have revived his former contacts."

"IM Maggot? Stasi?"

"You're from Western Germany, Neumeier. Therefore, you don't understand. You've no idea how things were back then. The old networks, they still exist. We might be getting on in years, but many of us are still around."

"I don't know what you're talking about."

"I'm starting to wonder if these strange worms might be the products of some secret military research project from those days."

There was a knock on the door of the faction hall. When the Chancellor gave a slight nod, the security men allowed the Parliamentary Party Leader to enter.

"I've something to report," the man said.

"Go ahead."

"Your people has come. It has assembled on the Platz der Republik."

"My people!" The Chancellor smiled. "My loyal subjects. See, Neumeier? That's what I've told you all along. Not all is lost yet. My people has come to protect me." The Chancellor stood, approaching the Party Leader with a smile on his face.

"Your enthusiasm might be a bit premature, I fear," the man replied. "There's definitely something wrong here."

"What do you mean?"

"Your people—it has turned into a frenzied mob."

9.

Inside the Holocaust Memorial

"They're still here," Frank said, supporting himself on the edge of his concrete stele to peer down into the narrow aisles between the monoliths. He looked over to Sophia who sat there, legs crossed. She had torn a piece off her sheet to create a cover for her head which she had loosely secured around her neck with a length of the strap of her shoulder bag. For Can, who had found a perch on the neighboring stele, she had fashioned a similar piece of headgear. Kai wore a garbage bag from the One-Euro store with three holes for his eyes and mouth. They had been able to stop the bleeding on the back of Can's head with the help of a number of tissues. However, not even the Aspirins from Frank's pocket could relieve his headache.

"They just won't go away, even if they can't see our faces," Frank stated. He was still wearing the cheap gas mask from the souvenir booth and was sweating miserably underneath it. With the grunting Zombies milling about below him in the vast memorial ground, he felt like a movie extra, having to wear a latex mask in a low-budget sci-fi flick.

"They're getting more and more," Sophia observed horrified.

"Well," Frank said. "Islamists plus converts. That's what exponential growth is all about, I guess."

"They need an external stimulus, someone who lures them away. There aren't any more people left for them to bite," Sophia replied.

"Something, like a bait, sort of?" Kai asked.

"A bait, right," she confirmed.

"I volunteer," Frank offered. "I'm sick and tired of this fucking mask anyway." He raised his iron bar, waving it high in the air. "I'll take some of these bastards down with me."

"Why don't you cool it? We need a plan, otherwise the distraction won't help us a thing," Sophia interjected.

"Shang needs a doc," Kai said.

"Oh, he's doing fine," Frank waved him off. "He just passed out for a couple of minutes."

"But I'm feeling sick," Can protested.

"A concussion, maybe," Sophia speculated.

"What matters is whether he has amnesia," Frank replied. "Is there anything you can tell us about your friends down there? About what they want? Anything ring a bell?"

"I remember… I remember… what an asshole you are."

"See?" Frank seemed to be satisfied. "It's all still there."

"Just cut out this bickering!" Sophia scolded. "The situation is bad enough as it is. What are we going to do now?"

"Well, maybe Can really needs to see a doc," Frank conceded. "Charité Hospital is not too far from here."

"How far?" Can asked, sounding miserable.

Frank took out is phone to start Google Maps, but there still was no signal. "About a mile, I guess," he finally replied.

"In his state he won't make it," Sophia doubtfully said.

"I could carry him," Kai offered. "No problem. I'm just not supposed to lift anything. Doctor's orders. Carrying's okay."

"Right, then let's go to Pariser Platz and from there to Charité," Frank declared, pointing the way with his metal bar.

Frank and Sophia lifted Can on Kai's back.

"I'll lure our Quran thumpers a bit further south and follow you then," Frank outlined his plan.

Sophia nodded.

Frank pulled off his gas mask. He jumped on the next stele over and beat his metal bar against its edge. "Come on, move it!" he

67

yelled at the Zombies, mingling below. "Step up, it's feeding time. Another infidel to convert." When he continued leaping from stele to stele, the Zombies began to fall in step after him. "Come on!" he called, arms spread wide and sounding almost relieved. "Here I am, the last man standing. Just take me into the folds of your community. I can hardly wait to be enlightened by your glorious religion."

"He actually seems to enjoy himself," Sophia commented.

"That's the good thing about being a nutcase," Can mumbled, his voice still filled with pain. "Even a Zombie Apocalypse can't hurt you."

"He's the Scout," Kai hushed him. "He'll show us the way."

When the three reached the northern end of the steles, they turned. About a hundred yards away from them, Frank was still jumping from stele to stele, while lashing out with his bar at his opponents. He seemed to have a good time, keeping the Zombies in hot pursuit. When Sophia waved at him, he didn't even notice her. Soon, he was dancing along the lower steles, allowing the Zombies to touch him like a rock star basking in the adoration of his frenzied fans.

He scooted back to the higher steles in the middle of the memorial. When he finally happened to look in Sophia's direction, she began waving again and motioned him over. Frank twirled his iron bar like a baton. "Coming!" he yelled.

Can clinging on to his back, Kai turned into Wilhelmstrasse. The area in front of the British Embassy was blocked off with bollards.

"You!" an amplified voice resounded. "Come here!"

"Who's that?" Sophia wondered aloud.

"It's coming from over there." Kai pointed at the Embassy building.

"From the Embassy?"

"Enter through the door and you'll be safe," the amplified voice started again.

"Look. The little door over there has opened," Sophia said. "Weird. It must be some kind of service entrance."

Meanwhile, Frank had joined them. After he had put on his gas mask again, the Zombies had left him alone. "Come on!" he urged, pointing where Charité Hospital was.

"Maybe they'll help us here," Sophia ventured, approaching the open door, camouflaged by the slats of a ventilation system. Kai followed with Can still on his back. After casting a doubtful look around, Frank also stepped through the door, which immediately slammed shut behind him.

The four walked down a narrow hallway, completely lined with aluminum foil, passing a grid that housed a maze of pipes and shafts. The corridor ended at a wall. A fluorescent light source, a camera, and a loudspeaker were attached to the ceiling. A number of benches were lined up along the side walls. Aided by Sophia, Kai carefully lowered Can on one of them.

"Is this supposed to be their visitors' center?" Frank asked, his tone incredulous.

"This place can't be Embassy territory." Sophia shook her head.

"Well," Frank retorted. "The English aren't known for their hospitality."

"I'm the Prepper," a voice from the speaker announced.

"Hi," Kai said, waving into the camera. "I've always wanted to meet you."

"Prepper?" Sophia repeated.

Frank grinned. "Always be prepared. Preppers are people who want to be ready when the apocalypse comes," he explained.

"What?"

"It's some kind of online community. You plan ahead what types of food and other equipment you need to stock up on, if you want to survive the collapse of our civilization."

"What do you have to offer?" the Prepper continued.

"Offer?" Sophia couldn't believe what she was hearing. She pulled the sheet off her head.

"I'm talking about tradable items," the Prepper clarified.

"What's wrong with you?" Frank asked, exasperated. "You must have been watching *Mad Max* too much."

"Times have changed."

"After just five hours of apocalypse? What, are you crazy?"

"You need shelter and food," the Pepper went on, unperturbed.

"Well, we don't need anything from you, I guess," Frank retorted. "There is a little One-Euro store on Friedrichstrasse, run by a very resolute lady."

Kai laughed. "Yeah, and there's also baby Rita locked up in the john."

"I'm surrounded by nutcases," Can groaned. He took off his sheet to rub his temple. "I should've joined my brothers fighting ISIS. Everything's better than this shit here."

"Your brothers are fighting against ISIS?" Frank was surprised. "Hats off."

"Yeah, they went to Iraq, but they refused to take me along," Can explained.

"What are they fighting in Iraq for? You're all Germans, right?" Sophia was confused.

Can looked up to them. "You're acting like a German, that's what my brothers used to say to me. Too soft. A simpering jellyfish and a disgrace to our family."

"You're not a jellyfish," Sophia protested.

"You might not be Mr. Hulk," Frank agreed, "but the fact that we're still alive we only owe to your burka trick. You're not a bodybuilding type, but when in war you also need to keep your

70

wits together. Brawn and brains," Frank insisted, touching a finger to his forehead.

"Are you sure?" Can asked.

"Yeah," Frank and Sophia confirmed as one.

Kai sat on the bench next to Can, putting an arm around his shoulder. "You're our Juggler," he said.

Can smiled. "And you, my friend, you're the Wrestler."

"Wrestler?" Kai repeated.

"The man who can catch a Zombie and hold her in a headlock, without showing fear."

"The Wrestler," Kai said, a sparkle in his eyes. He looked at Frank.

"Whatever Can says," he replied.

"That's great!" the Prepper announced. "People bonding when the going gets tough. I need to write this down." Static could be heard. After a while the Prepper's voice came back. "You're giving each other battle names. That's even better."

"And what's your name supposed to mean?" Frank asked. "The Prepper? Been playing too much *ZombiU*, right?"

"*ZombiU*?" Sophia asked.

Kai and Frank exchanged a knowing glance.

"An old console game," Frank explained. "It's about a Zombie Apocalypse taking place in London and it also features a Prepper who pulls the strings in the background."

"What exactly does he do?" Sophia wanted to know.

"He uses other people for his own advantage. They're all dead in the end," Frank said, looking into the camera. "You can't trust this guy."

"He has an important job to do," the Prepper protested.

"Your idol just wants to save his own neck. How nobel of him," Frank sneered. "That's the kind of guy you wanna be?"

"I haven't…," the Prepper began, "… I haven't invited you in to argue with you."

"Then just let us leave," Frank shot back, walking to the door. "Everything out there is better than to talk to a cheating snake like you are."

"What do you want from us?" Sophia asked.

"What I want? Information on what's going on out there."

"Just take a look out of the window," Frank suggested.

"What is it you want to know?" Sophia asked.

"There's no more internet. Are these really the ISIS butchers I've been reading about?"

"People have been infected with an illness. It's some kind of parasite," Sophia replied.

"*Puleeeze!* They're fucking Islamist mutants," Frank groaned.

"There're Germans among them. People of all religions and skin colors," Sophia insisted.

"Spare me this PC gibberish. These people have been converted against their free will."

"Converted?" the Prepper wanted to know.

"Yeah. One bite, and *poof* - reason and independent thinking fly right out of the window," Frank confirmed.

"What are you talking about?" the Prepper said.

"Don't listen to him, Herr... Prepper. This man is confused," Sophia protested.

"Confused? It all started with the Islamists, right? That's a fact," Frank defended himself.

"Because we happened to be in Kreuzberg. In Marzahn it would have been the Nazis who attacked us."

"Because everyone living in Marzahn is a Nazis? Wow, what an enlightened, unbiased view," Frank scoffed, his voice dripping with sarcasm.

"But they aren't Islamists," Sophia continued to fight back. "These people have been infested."

"Here she goes again, balancing opinions."

"I'm not! I'm only saying that it could also have started with Germans."

"Maybe... maybe you're right. Another explanation might be that Islamism has just entered into a perfect symbiosis with wormhood."

"*Worms*? What the hell are you talking about?" the Prepper interrupted.

"It looks as if some kind of leech has made its home in people's brains and now influences their behavior," Sophia clarified.

"It's their religion controlling their behavior," Frank insisted, albeit half-heartedly.

"A worm that makes people lose their minds?" the Prepper demanded. "How come?"

"*Dicrocoelium dendriticum*," Sophia replied.

"What?"

"It's a phenomenon that we know already exists in nature," Sophia explained. "A tiny liver fluke latches on to the spinal ganglion of an ant and proceeds to manipulate its host. It convinces the ant that it is a good idea to sit on the tip of a blade of grass, where it is then eaten by a sheep, making it the next intermediate host."

"Dicro...?"

"*Dicrocoelium dendriticum*."

"Pity I can't look it up online," the Prepper regretted. "But I can ask others if they've ever heard of it."

"Do you have phone reception?" Frank asked.

"No, just CB radio," the Prepper answered. "Do you know how to stop this worm?"

"You bash the guy's head in until it bursts, and then the worms come squirting out," Kai suggested.

"Another way is to fool them," Can, who had meanwhile picked himself up, added. "The infection carriers react to human faces. Therefore, wearing a mask offers some protection."

73

"You guys are really good," the Prepper declared. "A functioning team needs to unite a wide range of abilities."

"You need to pass on the info," Frank instructed. "It might encourage people who're still laying low in their houses to fight back."

"Will do," the Prepper promised.

"And don't forget to mention who the info comes from."

"I'll post the video online. That is, as soon as I have a signal again."

Kai smiled into the camera. "Cool," he said.

"Do you happen to know anyone in Kassel?" Frank suddenly asked.

"Kassel?"

"That's where my family lives."

"Or in Tübingen?" Sophia added.

"No, we're all from Berlin," the Prepper replied.

"What, if the situation there is the same as here?" Sophia gave Frank a worried glance.

"You've just said that the ant is only the fluke's intermediate host," the Prepper began.

Sophia nodded, yes. "That's right."

"If this makes us humans intermediate hosts, too, who, the hell might then be the final host?"

"No idea." Sophia mulled over the question. "Maybe we just ended up on its menu by accident. The worm normally might seek out different hosts."

"But why now of all times? Why hasn't it happened earlier?"

"There are thousands of parasitic worms on this planet. It might have been around for a long time already and simply remained under the radar of science."

"Could it be due to climate change? Might the worm come from Africa?" the Prepper insisted.

"I've honestly no idea," Sophia admitted.

"Well," the Prepper left it at that. "You've definitely earned yourselves a reward." In the wall at the narrow end of the corridor a hatch opened at chest-level, revealing eight energy bars, four cans of cola, a flare, and a torch. Frank reached for two cans, tossing one to Kai and the other to Can. When he offered the third one to Sophia, she declined. He opened his can and drained it.

"Do you happen to have a Bionade?" Sophia asked into the camera.

"What?"

"Forget it, that's an organic soda," Frank said, distributing the energy bars. Then he pointed at the flare and the torch. "What are those supposed to be for?"

"You'll need them," the Prepper said.

"Why?"

"You'll have to do me a favor."

"Wait a minute. We've given you information. Now, we're even."

"I've given you food, after all."

"I wouldn't go so far as to call some cola and energy bars food. I could also nick them from a vending machine."

"But you need to help me."

"We don't need to do anything," Frank protested.

"What do you want?" Sophia interjected.

"I'm looking for someone."

"Welcome to the club," Frank scoffed.

"But my little sister is here in Berlin, not somewhere in Germany."

"Your little sister?" Sophia repeated.

"I've lost contact to her. She also owns a CB radio, but she doesn't answer it."

"Where is she?" Sophia wanted to know.

Frank shook his head. "You seriously want to help him?"

"At the Move Inn Hotel on Alexanderplatz," the Prepper replied.

"That's not far from here, right?" Sophia said.

"Not true during a Zombie Apocalypse, when you have to multiply every foot by ten. We also have more important things to do." Frank was adamant.

"Like looting?" Can joked.

"Great suggestion," Frank laughed.

"Where exactly is your little sister?", Sophia asked.

"Rebecca is inside the panorama restaurant," the Prepper answered.

"Ok, I'll look for your little sister." Sophia's mind was made up.

"Don't do anything stupid," Frank warned. "We wanted to go to Charité Hospital."

"And what reason do we have to worry about this guy's problems?" Can came to his aid. "We don't even know his agenda."

"I'll go anyhow," Sophia insisted. "Also without you, if I need to. I can't leave a little girl to her fate."

"You're a great person," the Prepper thanked her. "I've no idea what I'd do if something happened to her. She's all I've left."

"If you tell people how to protect themselves, we'll help you to look for your little sister," Frank grudgingly agreed. "But if this is a trick, we'll sic a gang of Zombies on you. Then, even your stupid aluminum wallpaper won't save you."

"You won't regret it. I swear," the Prepper promised.

"I hope so," Frank replied, not quite convinced.

"Take the flare and the torch."

"We won't need them. It's barely three o'clock in the afternoon. Night's still a long way off."

"Right. But you'll need to go underground."

"What?"

"Down into the subway tunnel. The new U5 track."

"But it isn't finished yet."

"The tunnel's already there, allowing you to walk all the way from Brandenburger Tor to Alexanderplatz. There aren't any tracks yet and the stations are still under construction. The odds are that you won't meet anyone down there."

"Besides the workers."

"Yeah, maybe them."

"But it's safer than the streets in any case."

"You might be right. Unter den Linden must be swarming with our bearded friends," Frank admitted.

The fluorescent light went off, only to click back on a second later.

"What was that?" Sophia wanted to know.

"Power failure. The emergency generators have kicked in," the Prepper explained. "I'll now show you the way." One of the grids on the floor magically opened, exposing stairs leading down. "There's an auxiliary passage, connecting it with the main tunnel."

"Which direction?" Frank asked.

"There's only way to go. You can't get lost."

Sophia hesitated. "Down? Do you really think that's a good idea?"

"Why not?" Frank said, turning to Can. "You'd better stay here to get some rest."

"No way, I'll stay behind with this madman," Can protested. "I'm coming along."

"You're barely able to walk straight."

"Kai can support me," Can suggested.

"Ok," Kai agreed.

"Then let's go," Frank ordered.

The four walked down the stairs and followed a corridor lined by a number of pipes. It ended at a metal door, where the key was in the lock. They opened it and unlocked it behind them. Frank pocketed the key.

Sophia pointed the torch into the blackness. In front of them there was the unfinished tunnel of U5, which, in a year from now, would connect Honow with Hauptbahnhof, the central train station.

"You think the Prepper can be trusted?", Sophia asked, shining the light along the slabs of concrete formwork.

"He seems to be a coward," Frank mused.

"They all were dead, after the Prepper talked to them," Kai said.

Frank turned to him. "You're talking about *ZombiU*?"

"He didn't give a shit."

"It was only a game," Sophia pointed out. "I'm sure our Prepper is different."

"People pulling the strings in the background always have something to hide," Frank stated.

"Do you hear this?" Can interrupted, fearfully peering into the darkness.

"What?" Sophia asked.

"These weird noises behind us."

The four turned around, Sophia pointing the torch into the night. Now, they all were able to hear the strange sounds, echoing off the tunnel's walls. However, there was nothing to be seen in the beam of their torch.

"What is this?" Sophia asked, shining the torch into Frank's eyes.

"No idea. It's quite loud. Sounds like someone snorting and sniffing."

"Sniffing?"

"Well, like… like hundreds of dogs trying to pick up a scent."

Frank took the flare, lit it, and tossed it as far as he could into the tunnel. The torch hit the ground, bathing its surroundings in a reddish light. But when the four tried to make out any movement, there still was nothing. The strange noises seemed to be coming closer.

"Let's split." Sophia was whispering, even though they seemed to be alone.

"We have to find out who's following us," Can protested. The eerie sounds were fast approaching. Transfixed, the four were staring at the flare, whose fire seemed to burn brighter when a shadow appeared on the tunnel's ceiling. Soon, there was a second one. And a third one.

"Oh, my God," Sophia breathed. A band of Zombies was robot-walking straight at them. The ones in the first row were moving on all fours, their noses down to the ground like track dogs. The others behind them held themselves more or less upright. From time to time they threw their heads back, taking deep breaths, as if they, too, were trying to sniff out their prey.

"They can't see anything down here. That's why they're sniffing," Frank deduced.

Can pulled the sheet off his head. "In this case we can forget about our disguise."

Kai offered him his arm, and then the four of them started running. The flare petered out. There was nothing but the harsh breathing sounds, behind them in the dark. The beam of the torch skittered across concrete walls, feeling its way along scaffolding until it landed on the wooden steps, connecting the tunnel to the next level. They seemed to have reached one of the stations, still under construction. Kai climbed the stairs first, holding on to Can who had trouble staying on his feet. Sophia followed, with Frank bringing up the rear. When they arrived at mezzanine level, they noticed concrete steps leading up to the street. Through a crack in the structure light was streaming in.

"I'll stand my ground," Frank suddenly declared.

"What are you talking about?" Sophia wanted to know.

"I'll face these bastards. I refuse to stay in hiding any longer. Somebody has to fight these Zombie Islamists."

"Are you crazy? Come on. The exit's up there!" Can urged. "We've almost made it."

Kai let go of Can, nodding his head. "I'm staying, too."

"No, my friend," Frank said. "You go with Sophia. You guys have to get to the Move Inn. Rebecca has a CB device. You can use it to radio for help."

"You have to come with us. We need you," Sophia pleaded.

"There's no going back for me. They'll never leave us alone just like this. I refuse to run."

Meanwhile, the first Zombies had reached the wooden stairs and continued their clumsy march up.

"I wish you luck." Frank turned away from his friends, raised his metal bar, and started walking down the steps straight at the approaching Zombies. The shaft of light coming in from the street illuminated the middle of the staircase, where Frank stopped and waited. "Come on, bastards. Here I am!" he taunted the Zombies, beating the railing with his metal bar. Blinded by the light, the first Zombie stopped and seemed to assess him. Frank slammed the bar into his forehead. The Zombie staggered backwards and toppled down the stairs. The second and the third Zombie also collapsed, felled by Frank's blows on their heads, bodies, and legs. "I'll teach you what it means to mess with us!" he screamed, kicking a Zombie in the second wave of attackers straight in the face. He felt a squirt of liquid connecting with his own face, but he didn't care. Like Leonidas and the Thermopylae, the thought shot through his head. That's how he was going to defend this bottleneck. It was out of the question to withdraw. These bastards were going to pay. Here and now. Just that it wasn't three hundred Spartans fighting a multitude of foes, but just one single man.

10.

There was a burning sensation in Mustermann's swollen forehead. No matter how hard he rubbed, the pain just wouldn't go away. When he pressed his fingers against it, he was able to force the protrusion back into his skull, but the bulge returned as soon as he removed his hand. Was there any bone left? He definitely needed something to stabilize this thing.

You're almost there, the strange voice addressed him again.

What? Mustermann thought.

You've almost made it. Just look ahead.

Mustermann complied.

What do you see?

A square full of people.

You know that these aren't people any more.

But they still look like people.

They're now part of our community.

Community?

Don't you remember what I've told you?

I… not really.

You were weak and that's why they've left you behind.

They?

Our enemies.

I was weak?

You were weak, but we've given you strength. You were tortured by doubts, but we've shown you the way. You were lonely, but we've welcomed you in our community.

Yes, now I remember. I remember those who have betrayed me, pretending to be my friends. Who have abandoned me.

They are not your friends.

81

I know now.

We're not like them. We'd never abandon you.

But it hurts so much.

The pain won't last.

I can hardly control my legs.

You'll be able to use them as long as you need them.

But this pain...

Do you see the parasol over there? The tiny one you can wear on your head? It'll make your pain better.

Mustermann picked up the wearable parasol, left there by some tourist. The fabric had the color of the German flag. He pulled the plastic ring over the crown of his head and tightened it to hold his bulge in place.

Raise your head, the voice inside his mind was saying now.

Mustermann did it.

What do you see?

The Reichstag Building.

The doors are locked. But you still know how to get in.

Yes. There is a way.

Show our brothers this way. Because we are one. We all belong together.

11.

Rotes Rathaus, seat of the Governing Mayor of Berlin, station of subway line U5 (under construction)

The City Hall towered in front of them. The sky had opened its floodgates. The jubilant noises of Zombies celebrating their successful hunt wafted up from the dark tunnel under their feet, when a dazed Sophia, Kai, and Can made their way across the construction site. Eyes red and his face a mask of horror, Kai turned to Sophia. He was still supporting Can, whose legs kept on buckling under him from sheer exhaustion.

"Come on, don't slow down!" Sophia urged the others, pushing aside the fence that blocked off the construction site. Kai, who had his head turned sideways, walked straight into her.

"What?" Sophia asked, when she noticed the utter fear in his face. "What's wrong?" She followed his eyes. In the square in front of the construction site there were hundreds, maybe even thousands of Zombies, covering the ground. Their skulls had burst open. The rain was washing worms, white larvae, yellowish eggs, and the remains of brain-matter into the gutters. The Zombies's corpses filled the square all the way up to the TV tower and piled up in the water basin of Neptunbrunnen and on the pavement in front of Rotes Rathaus. Lifeless and all their rage and hatred spent, they gave a pathetic picture. When she heard a grunt from the subway tunnel below them, Sophia clung on to Kai's arm. Shoulder to shoulder and their throbbing bulges bared, the Zombies were pushing up the stairs to the station and started their swaying march in their direction. The three stopped, rooted to the spot. Suddenly, the Zombies began shaking their heads back and forth in a frenzy. One after another, they dropped to the ground, convulsing one last time before the bubbles on their foreheads burst wide open.

Kai wiped the raindrops off his face, laughing. "They're earthworms, after all," he said. "When it rains, they need to crawl out into the open."

"Yes," Can agreed. "Nothing but stupid earthworms."

"Biologically speaking these aren't…" Sophia started to protest. But then she put her head back, closed her eyes, and let the rain wash over her face. "They behave a bit like earthworms, don't they?"

"Earthworms always come crawling out when it rains," Kai confirmed.

At the foot of the TV tower a group of teens were using the situation to their best advantage by robbing the felled Zombies, taking their wallets, phones, and money. Other than these body-strippers there was no one else on the streets. Only on some the balconies of the high-rises surrounding the spacious square people stood, looking down. Some had beer bottles in their hands, others held their phones up into the sky, trying to get a signal. When they noticed the three friends, some of them called out. However, it wasn't cries for help. Can, Kai, and Sophia had no way of telling what these people might want from them. All the way to the elevated tracks of the local commuter train the street was covered with dead Zombies, their skulls split open. Worms were writhing on tarmac, in desperate search of a new host. Their clothes soaking wet, the three reached the foyer of Move Inn Hotel. The reception desk was deserted and nobody stopped them on their way to the elevators.

"They still have electricity," Can wondered aloud. When he pressed the call button, the cage started its descent from the 37th floor.

"They must have their own emergency generator," Sophia speculated.

"Might the whole thing be over, after all?" Can was hopeful.

"No, it's not," Kai replied, pointing at the five Zombies, who came staggering from the room behind the desk. A ping announced the arrival of the elevator. When the door opened, there was an old lady in a wheelchair inside the cage.

"What the hell? Is she…?" Can asked.

"No, she's just having a nap," Kai said. He moved the chair with the old lady in it into a corner of the cage to make room for all of them. Sophia quickly pressed button "37". But the first Zombie reached the elevator before the door had closed. Kai blocked the access to the cage with his massive body, but with the Zombie in the way of the light barrier the door wouldn't shut. The Zombie reached out for Kai, trying to dig his fangs into his neck, but didn't stand a chance as his intended victim towered over him. With a hard shove Kai pushed the Zombie away.

"Up! We need to go up!" Can yelled, while Sophia was frantically pummeling button "37". Two more Zombies moved in for the kill. "No, no!" Sophia screamed.

Suddenly, Frank appeared behind the attackers, rushed one of them, and dug a putty knife into his forehead.

"Scoouut!" Kai called out. "The Scout is back!"

Frank went for the next Zombie, driving his putty knife into the worm-filled bladder with deadly precision. The other two Zombies still ignored him, opting to go at Kai instead. Frank also popped their worm-reservoirs. Sophia just stood there, staring agape. Can's face was a mask of fear. Only Kai was smiling. "The Scout is back!" he cheered again.

Frank's face was devoid of emotion. He had tied one of the green bandanas, taken from one of the Zombie-Salafists, around his neck. He pulled the lifeless bodies of the Zombies free from the door in a leisurely pace and boarded the elevator.

"Frank?" Sophia couldn't believe it. "How did you…? How have you…?"

"Gotten away?" Frank lowered his eyes. Soft elevator music started to play. "Isn't it enough that I'm here?"

Kai slapped Frank's shoulder. "You've made it."

"You think I'm gonna let a bunch of crazies do me in?"

Can gave Frank a critical once-over. "What happened to your neck?"

"Just a bite…"

"A *bite?*" Can jumped back.

"Maybe two," Frank corrected himself. "Haven't looked into a mirror yet."

When Sophia wanted to touch the bandana, Frank pushed her hand away. "It's nothing," he said.

"Wouldn't you be…?" Sophia pensively started. "Wouldn't you be…?"

"Wouldn't I be what?"

"Be turned by now?"

"You know what?" Frank replied with a tortured smile, "Maybe those worms simply don't stand a chance with agnostics like me."

"What's this stink?" Kai was waving his hand in front of his nose.

"It smells really awful," Sophia agreed.

"What are you looking at me for?" Frank protested. "It's your new friend over here." He pointed at the wheelchair lady.

"I don't believe it." Kai held his nose.

"Did the old bird fart on us?" Can turned away in disgust.

"Oh, man," Kai said. "The quiet ones are often the biggest stinkers."

"As if this horrible muzak wasn't enough," Frank complained. "Who is she, by the way?"

"No idea. She was sleeping inside the elevator when we got here," Kai explained.

When the cage stopped on the 37th floor, Frank was the first to get out. "You stay here. I'll check out the lay of the land," he said, blocking the door with a chair. Brandishing his putty knife, he began searching the panorama café for Zombies. When he had convinced himself that there weren't any worm-carriers around, he took a seat at the bar. "The coast is clear. You can come in!" he called over to the others. Then, he rapped on the wood. "You don't need to hide anymore either."

"Who are you talking to?" asked Sophia, when she joined Frank.

"The young lady who ducked behind the bar, when we arrived."

A girl came up behind the bar, showing Frank the finger. Her face was painted white with faint outlines of cobwebs around her eyes. She wore faded jeans and balanced a longboard in one hand. *I want to leave*, said the legend on her hoodie below a UFO shape. The desire to leave the earth seemed to be a variation on *I want to believe*, the motto of the Alien community, Frank thought. "Great, a fourteen-year-old nihilist," he said with a wide grin. "You're Rebecca, I assume."

The girl raised a brow. "Whaddaya talking about?"

"I'm sure you must be the Prepper's little sister."

"Prepper? What Prepper?"

"Isn't he your brother?"

"Not that I know of."

"Who are you, then?"

"None of your business."

"It's okay to tell us your name," Sophia said.

"Yes, we want to help you," Can added.

"I can take care of myself."

"Sure. Just like all teenagers of this world," Frank scoffed.

"Fuck you."

"How do you want us to call you then? Jackie, the Skater-Girl?" Frank continued to taunt her.

Again, the girl presented him with her middle digit.

"Sorry, you must be the dark edition, a badass Skater-Girl, right?"

"Stop harassing her," Sophia intervened.

"What's bothering you?" Frank asked. "We're having a great time, the two of us. We're bonding."

"We're here on an important assignment from the Prepper," Kai announced, his tone brimming with importance as if on the quest for the Holy Grail.

"Assignment?" the girl repeated.

"We need to find Rebecca. The Prepper's little sister. Then, he'll give us food and allow us to use his radio, right?"

"Don't kill the messenger, but I think someone played a real sick joke on you," the girl said.

"What are we going to do with the old lady from the elevator?" Can asked.

"I've totally forgotten about her," Sophia admitted.

"Well, the more the merrier," Frank declared. "Do you want to get her, Kai?"

"I can do it," Can offered.

"Are you okay again?" Frank asked.

"I'm still a bit wobbly, but I also want to make myself useful." Can went to get the old lady and rolled her wheelchair up to the bar.

Sophia eyed Frank's neck. "Why are you wearing a bandana? What happened? And how have you managed to survive?"

"You're curious, right?"

"We have a right to know the truth."

"It seems to have paid off that I've watched *Taxi Driver* five times. The perfect preparation for an apocalypse, that much I can tell you."

"You're pretty retro, right?" Can joked.

"Let me have a look," insisted Sophia, reaching for the bandana. Frank tried to push her away at first, but eventually let her remove the cloth. Even though his neck showed a number of deep teeth marks, the main arteries were intact. "No blood, in spite of all these wounds," she stated amazed.

"These worms must be issuing some substance that stops the bleeding," Frank speculated. "It doesn't hurt either."

"What happened to you down there in the tunnel?" Can insisted.

"Well, I've neutralized... killed a number of Zombies, don't know what the right word is," Frank replied matter-of-factly. "I vented all my hatred and taught them a lesson. One after the other. I stepped over their bodies, smashing their skulls with my metal bar. However, my hatred wasn't enough for all of them. Eventually they got me. Afterwards I must have been out of it for a while. No idea what happened during this time. When I picked myself up, I was surrounded by Zombies. But they had stopped attacking me."

"You've vented your hatred? Didn't you feel any sympathy for this people?"

"They stopped being people a long time ago. Now, they're nothing but humanoids in attack-mode. Them or us. Survival is the only thing that counts. It doesn't matter what they used to be. Of course I feel sorry for what has become of them," he added, looking at Sophia. "And just to make you happy: It didn't give me any pleasure to batter these bastards to kingdom come."

Sophia turned to Kai. "Why don't you check, if there's a first-aid-kit in the kitchen. It's probably hanging on the wall."

"It's just a scratch," Frank waved her off.

"And you, pass me the whiskey, please" Sophia addressed the girl. "And tell me your name."

"Claudia. The name's Claudia." She handed Sophia the bottle.

"I need to disinfect the wound."

"Disinfect? First things first," Frank protested. "First, I have to cleanse myself from the inside." Frank eyed the bar. "Free choice of poison, I guess. Sadly, no bartender."

"When there's a party I'm always in charge of the cocktails," Can offered.

"You?" Frank was incredulous. "I've always thought Muslims don't drink."

"I only mix the drinks. The drinking part I leave up to the others."

"It takes all kinds. Let's hope that Allah'll turn a blind eye."

"Don't you worry about him."

"Ok. Can you do a mojito for me?"

"No prob." Can stepped behind the bar, arranged rum and lime juice in front of him, and took fresh mint leaves from the fridge. Meanwhile, Kai had returned from the small kitchen, carrying a first-aid-kit. Sophia took out a pad, soaked it in whiskey and carefully dabbed at the gaping wound.

"It still doesn't hurt." Frank was surprised. "Not at all."

"That's weird." Sophia studied the wound, rubbing the pad across it. "There's something stuck in there."

"What the hell are you talking about?" Frank ground out.

"A foreign object. Something black," Sophia explained.

Frank gulped down the mojito Can had served him in one swig. "Fuck!"

"I'll make you another one, brother," Can offered.

Sophia was thinking. "I've an idea. I've watched a documentary about the Amazon region some time ago. About how people there deal with parasites. Hold on." She disappeared into the kitchen, returning with a bottle of oil.

"You wanna fry me now?" Frank drawled. "Aren't there any less radical solutions to the problem? I'm offering to apologize for every insult that ever crossed my lips."

"It's a bit late for than," Sophia joined the banter.

"But I still beg your pardon: To go cannibal on the first day of a Zombie Apocalypse? Aren't you laying it on too strong? What's the slogan on your bag again? *Go vegan*? Doesn't this include human flesh?"

Sophia shook her head in exasperation. "You and your silly jokes."

"I'm sure you've missed them."

"Maybe a little," Sophia confessed. She soaked a pad in oil and dabbed the wound with it. Then, she took the bottle and started to pour oil directly over the cut.

"Hey, you're messing up my clothes," Frank complained.

"Don't move," Sophia ordered. She inspected the wound, formed her fingers into a pair of tweezers, and tweaked it.

"Are you nuts?" Frank exploded, even though he hadn't felt any pain. Actually, he didn't feel a thing.

Sophia started pulling a black object from the wound. It was so slippery, that she had to adjust her grasp a few times. Finally, she tossed a black worm onto the bar and squashed it with the whiskey bottle.

"Uggh, that's gross!" Claudia turned away in revulsion.

Frank studied the flattened worm. "How did you... how did you know...?"

"In order to stay alive under your skin, a worm needs to breathe. To this effect it everts its breathing apparatus, which can then be sealed with oil, forcing it to come up if it doesn't want to suffocate."

"Oh, my goodness, you really know a lot," Frank said with grudging admiration.

"Knowledge is power," Sophia deadpanned. She used the pad to wipe the excess oil off and then pressed a clean one to the wound. "Hold on to it," she ordered. He complied, while she unspooled two lengths of adhesive strip and used them to affix the bandage to the skin.

Kai observed her in awe. "Now we know what your name is, right?" he declared.

"What are you talking about?" Sophia said.

"You're the Doc."

"What? No! I just...," Sophia protested.

"Yes, you're our Doc now."

Frank nodded, yes. "Yes, I vote for granting you a medical-board approved license." Unable to express his gratitude, he just looked at Sophia. Then he pulled the pair of handcuffs taken along from the apartment on Mehringplatz from his pocket.

"What do you want with those?" Sophia asked.

"I can't stay with you," Frank explained. "I'm a danger to you. Only heaven knows why I haven't started to turn yet."

"Maybe I've removed the worm in time."

"Maybe it had already begun laying eggs."

"Eggs," Can repeated, wrinkling his nose. "I think I need a stiff drink now." He poured himself a whiskey and downed it.

"Allah won't mind, I guess," Frank said, toasting him with his second glass of mojito, and drained it. "I'll go up to the roof and chain myself to something there. You barricade the doors to the staircase and block all the elevators."

"Why do we still have electricity here? There's a power failure almost everywhere else in the city."

"This is the former Interhotel." The wheelchair lady's hectoring voice caused Sophia to jump. The woman opened her eyes and cleared her throat. "In the German Democratic Republic

Interhotels were equipped with state-of-the-art technology," she continued.

"German Democratic Republic? That's ancient, right?" Frank commented.

"Would you mind pouring me a little drink, young man?" the old woman addressed Can.

When Can held out a bottle of plum brandy, she nodded, yes. Can filled a glass for her. "Why don't you chain yourself up down here?" he suggested to Frank.

"No, I'd rather not," Frank answered. "I want to be alone right now. I need a little time to myself. Who knows for how long I'll be able to keep my wits together."

"You don't have to go," Sophia insisted. "You can stay with us."

"He's the Scout," Kai said. "A man goes where he needs to go."

Frank nodded, yes. "Yeah, he's right." He rose, walked over to the staircase, climbed the steps, and opened the door leading to the roof.

The sun had gone down, and Frank was looking down on the city of Berlin. The neon sign of Move Inn Hotel still worked, but most of the other buildings were dark. An occasional scream, the barking of a dog, and the honk of a car horn could be heard on the streets. All the way over in Kreuzberg an apartment building seemed to be on fire. However, the fire engines' sirens remained silent. Whiskey bottle in hand, Frank was gazing at the moon, wondering how much time he had left.

The door to the staircase opened and Sophia appeared, carrying a couple of blankets. "That's the advantage of picking a hotel for a hiding place," she said.

"You need to be careful when entering the rooms," Frank said, his tone almost protective.

"There were no Zombies around."

"Still. Next time you'd better say something. Then I'll do it."

93

"I brought you some blankets."

"Thanks, but I'm not cold."

"Maybe now you you're not." Sophia put the blankets down on the balustrade.

"Are Zombies cold-blooded or warm-blooded, what do you think?" Frank asked.

"What?"

"Their skin feels warm to the touch, but they still emanate coldness somehow."

"You're not a Zombie!"

"Not yet." When Frank looked at her he saw the reflection of the moon in her eyes.

Sophia averted her eyes. "Have you noticed the stars?" she asked.

"Yeah."

"I've never seen them like this since I've moved here."

"That's because tonight almost the entire city is dark. No light pollution."

"Have you decided on a place to sleep yet? I mean, something where you can, you know…"

"Chain myself down? Under the neon sign, I guess," Frank replied. "It's a dry spot, at least."

"Frank?"

"Yeah?"

"What you did before…"

"What do you mean?"

"That you… that you did…"

"That I ran amok?"

"What you did for us… I wanted to thank you… Without you they'd have caught all of us."

"I only did what needed to be done."

"It was very courageous."

Frank smiled. "It had nothing to do with courage. That's the way men are."

"Please spare me your macho-crap."

Frank grinned. "Have you ever heard the story of the young mammoths?"

"What are you talking about?"

"During an excavation project, thousands of mammoth bones were discovered in a trench. All in layers on top of each other. The animals must have gotten stuck in a swamp over ten thousand years ago. Not all at once, mind you, but only a few at a time. Generation after generation. Until the swamp was full of them. Again and again a few of them were careless, daredevil, or simply crazy enough to just walk in there. Maybe they wanted to show off how cool they were."

"What are you trying to tell me?"

Frank looked Sophia into the eyes. "It was only young males who died there."

Sophia smiled. "What do you expect me to say?"

Frank turned away from Sophia. He supported himself on the balustrade, gazing down on the street below them. "Us guys, we're wired like this. We need to seek out danger. To test our limits. Testosterone's a real killer. Some of us are idiots and just stumble into trenches. And others are moronic enough to play hero and throw themselves at a horde of worm-infested Zombies to defend their friends. I'm glad to belong to group number two."

"We aren't mammoths, Frank. We don't tick like this."

"You know exactly that this isn't true. We haven't changed a bit during the last millenniums. We got a little more civilized, maybe. And grew larger brains that help us to handle our smartphones. But that's about it. Just take a look around you. How much of it, you think, will last for eternity?"

Sophia was silent.

"Why did you come up to the roof?" Frank asked.

"I wanted to make sure that you won't do anything stupid."

"That's all?"

"What more do you want?"

"Do you want me?" Frank didn't beat around the bush.

Sophia smiled. "Of course I do. I wanted you from the very beginning."

"So?"

"You've got the looks. What do I care what's going on behind this pretty face? The more depraved, the better."

"What?" Frank asked, incredulous.

"You don't seem to know much about women. The ways we find to adapt."

"You like me because you think I'm depraved?"

"I," Sophia began. But when she realized that Frank could hardly wait to hear her explanation, she took another deep breath to let him stew a bit. "I'll tell you a secret. A secret, passed on among women from generation to generation."

"Passed on? Like a secret society, you mean?"

"What did you think?"

"I was already worried that you might all be in collusion."

"I want you because you're genetically superior. It will improve the chances of survival for our children."

"Whoa, children? Just hold it right there!"

"A woman has to think ahead."

Frank frowned, studying her doubtfully. Then, a smile appeared on his face. "You know, Sophia, I've totally underestimated you."

"Let's hear it."

"I thought you had absolutely no sense of humor."

"And?"

"I was wrong, I guess."

Kai opened the door to the roof. Can and Claudia came right behind him. Blankets tucked under their arms, they slowly approached the balustrade.

"What did you do with the old woman?" Frank wanted to know.

"She's having a good time drinking at the bar," Can informed him. "Helping herself from the bottle of brandy I left with her."

"Well, let's set up camp for the night," Frank suggested. "Hulk is going to chain himself down now. You can watch his transformation from a safe distance."

12.

The next morning
Reichstag Building, a private side entrance facing River Spree

A Zombie, his head sporting a wearable parasol, threaded his way through the bodies littering the ground. He had to wade through worm-infested brain-matter that had collected in puddles on the tarmac. Hundreds of brothers, destroyed by the rain. Just this one Zombie had been spared, thanks to the waterproof protection of his unique headgear that had prevented his worms from being lured out on a suicidal exodus.

"Herr Undersecretary! Herr Undersecretary Mustermann!" one of the guards called out. He had opened a side entrance to the Reichstag Building and was waiting for his co-worker who, obviously under the erroneous assumption that the apocalypse was over, had gone out for a smoke.

"Come on, over here!" the guard called out again. The Zombie who had once been Mustermann did what he was told, a pattern of behavior that had been eternally engrained in his mind during his time as a person. Controlled by worms and a loyal, albeit unwitting, facilitator of President's plans, he now set out on his last mission. Which was to carry his diabolical seed into the Reichstag Building once and for all. His first step was sinking his teeth into the unsuspecting watchman's neck.

13.

"Are you still with us?" a voice asked.

"Yeah," Frank replied, opening his eyes. Sophia was right next to him, swaddled in a nest of blankets. When he noticed her relief because he hadn't turned overnight, he pressed a kiss on her forehead.

She smiled. "And how are you doing?" she wanted to know.

"I had lousy dreams," Frank replied.

"Small wonder."

"Of worms and stuff. I don't remember all the details, but I think I argued with their king."

"Their king?"

"The king of the worms."

Sophia yawned. "What did you argue about?"

"Religion."

"And what conclusions did you reach?"

"I was able to convince him that they were wrong and that Jihad could never win. That they'd lose everything. Then it was his turn to list all his reasons. Paradise, virgins, the usual. After he was done, I gave my closing statement. We then made a list of the pros and cons. And in the end I managed to convince him of my point of view. We had a drink together to celebrate, and finally he left with his entourage."

"And what exactly did you tell him?"

"If I only still knew. I can't remember."

"What a nuisance. We're very interested in your reasoning."

Frank touched a finger to his lips. "It's my blood, I think," he said.

"What are you talking about?"

"The reason why I didn't turn. I have thick blood. Antithrombin deficiency. It might work like a worm-repellant."

"You've got a genetic defect?"

"Yeah."

"Well, maybe the larvae really can't travel in your blood or…"

Frank stopped her. "No details, please."

"Okay, I'll shut up."

"You know what's the weirdest thing about it?" he said.

"What?"

"The fear I suffered in my dreams. Not of death, I mean. I wasn't afraid of dying, really. But of not being human any longer and still having to stay alive. A wanderer between the worlds."

"Sounds gruesome."

Frank studied the ground. "I've never been too fond of my own species. And still there was nothing that scared me more tonight than the notion of losing everything that's human about me."

Sophia caressed his cheek. "You know what? There's a nice breakfast waiting for us downstairs. We'll just sit at the window and have a cup of coffee."

Frank smiled. "If it weren't for women…"

"What about us?"

"Well, if it weren't for you, we'd be so totally lost."

"Why? Because you can't make your own coffee?"

"No, that's not what I wanted to say."

Sophia grinned mischievously.

Frank bit his lip. "Well, the new Sophia, the one with a sense of humor, needs some time to get used to." He stood, looking at his wrist in surprise. "Where are the handcuffs?"

"I took them off. They cut into your skin overnight."

"But I could have turned."

"You know what? Us women take risks, too."

"You really did that for me…" Frank broke off and swallowed.

Sophia rose to her feet. "Can and Claudia are already downstairs. Let's go join them."

"Wait a minute, I first need to talk to someone," Frank said, walking over to Kai. Kai sat on the balustrade, legs crossed, and was admiring the sunrise.

"It doesn't care," Kai said when he noticed that Frank was standing behind him.

"Come again?"

"The Sun. It doesn't care. It just rises. For people and Zombies alike. It doesn't give a shit…"

"Kai?"

"Yeah?"

"What was the real reason you were in this subway car? I mean, it was already eleven o'clock. Your work had started a long time ago."

"My mom always worries."

"You weren't going to work, right?"

"My boss says I'm dumb as shit. And I'm useless to him anyway 'cause my back is shot."

"I'm glad that your boss is an asshole."

"You're glad?"

"Otherwise you wouldn't have been on the train. And nobody would have saved me from the Zombies."

"Whaddaya mean?"

"You saved my life. You threw the train driver on the tracks. And it wasn't only me you saved. You carried Can all the way over here."

"Carry, I still can. Just not lift."

"In this new world, Kai, you're smart if you don't get yourself sick with worms. So what if people have told you you're useless so far? We need you. We won't make it without you."

"We still have to save my mom and dad, right?"

101

"We will, Kai, we will. We'll free this goddamn city from worms. We won't cower and hide. We'll be prepared and we'll fight back."

"Sounds great," Kai said, looking over to the TV tower.

The distant sound of helicopter rotors was quickly getting louder.

"I can't see any insignia," Frank said when the helicopters came into view.

"What?"

"These guys're not part of the German Armed Forces."

After flying two circles around the TV tower, the three helicopters landed next to the Neptunbrunnen. A unit of soldiers jumped out and started to secure the perimeter. When the Zombies attacked, the soldiers opened fire from automatic weapons. The first wave of opponents went down, but the second one managed to break through the defense line. The surviving soldiers hurried back into the helicopters. But only two of the three machines were able to lift off the ground.

"It looks like we have our work cut out for us," Frank observed matter-of-factly.

"We need more rain."

"Yeah, right. More rain." Frank slapped Kai's shoulder. "Are you coming?"

"In a moment."

"Okay, see you later."

"Yeah, see you later."

Frank turned away from Kai, following Sophia to the door that opened into the hallway, where Claudia had spray-painted the words "ISombies FUCK OFF" on the housing of the ventilation shaft.

"ISIS – I-Sombies," Frank mused. "When you see it written like this, it sums up the situation pretty accurately."

Sophia touched his shoulder. "Just don't get carried away again."

"You're right, but a guy needs to hold a grudge sometimes."

When they entered the panorama café, Can, Claudia, and the old women were sitting together at a table, having breakfast. Claudia was fiddling with the remote, trying to get a station on the TV above the bar.

"What's our next step?" Can asked.

"Depends," Frank replied. "We're still on a mission, right? We need to finish it, if we want the Prepper to help us."

"What business do *you* have with the Prepper?" the old lady demanded to know.

"What? You know the Prepper?" Can said.

"I do indeed. Herbert is my brother," the old lady explained.

"Your brother?" Sophia and Can repeated as one.

"Then you must be Rebecca," Frank exclaimed. "Do you happen to be younger than him?"

"As a matter of fact I am," Rebecca proudly replied.

"Man, the Prepper must be a hundred years old," Can observed.

"I'm still fit and strong, you little bugger," Rebecca shot back. "And my brother'll give you a piece of his mind when he gets here."

Suddenly, the TV came to life. "I've found a station," Claudia called out.

"Which one?" Can asked.

"This must be public television," Sophia assumed.

An improvised panel discussion was on air. The studio's back wall was taken up by a rainbow flag.

The head of the Green Party was tossing back his blond ponytail. "Let me start with a warm welcome our new Zombie citizens," he began. "Who, by wearing green bandanas on their

CO_2 neutral protest marches, are trying hard to become sustainable members of our ecological society. In order to make them feel more comfortable during their process of integration, I suggest that burkas should be worn by men and women alike to avoid insulting our newcomers' sensibilities." He gave a self-important cough. "I also advise the public to familiarize themselves with the updated list of micro aggression-triggering vocabulary, whose use is punishable by shitstorm from now on. As pronouncing these toxic words might have a re-traumatizing effect, I won't list them here but recommend that you look them up on our password-protected safe-to-use website instead."

The Leader of the Socialist Workers' Party straightened her red shirt that sadly clashed with her shining auburn mane of curls. "That's all very well," she took the floor, after clearing her throat. "But let's not forget that these Zombies also represent our new working class that needs to be integrated into the job market without delay, while passing legislation to avoid them being exploited by precarious forms of employment. No marching on Sundays, I say! What we also need is safe spaces that include no outdoor labor in case of rain."

During this exchange the Queer representative had been stroking their luxurious hipster bird with dainty fingers. "I'm being made invisible here. Again," they now declared. "True intercultural and gender equality can only be reached by amending the acronym LGBTQ with a Z, which will make it LGBTQZ from now on."

The others nodded wisely.

"Okay, people." The head of the Green Party called the meeting to order. "I think it's time to take a vote now. Who is in favor of proclaiming the Eco-Genderized Republic of Berlin right now?"

"Just wait a minute!" the representative of the PoC movement, who had been silent so far, interrupted. "Just because we aren't white, you've no right to act out your racism and leave us…"

"I've had it!" Claudia exclaimed, shutting off the TV.

"How can they just continue spouting the same bullshit as ever?" Sophia couldn't believe it.

"Playing to the camera is their life," Can sighed. "An apocalypse doesn't make a difference."

"At least it's official now," Frank grinned. "After my brush with Zombieism I'm an endangered species who needs to be protected from trauma at all costs."

Claudia laughed.

"Won't they ever leave us alone with their one-size-fits-all solutions?" Frank added.

"No, this madness will never stop," Can answered.

"You know what I think?" Frank asked the others.

"What?" Claudia said.

"That car racing isn't such a bad idea after all."

"What are you talking about?"

"I'm thinking of what Kai's dad does. When he's sick and tired of the whole spiel he simply goes to the races. The squealing of the tires and the roar of the engines drone out the chatter."

"Is there a racetrack nearby?" Sophia wanted to know.

Can nodded, yes. "The Avus counts as one, I guess. They used to have car races there in the old days. Today you could really burn rubber, because there won't be anyone around. All we need is a car."

"That shouldn't be too difficult." Frank smiled. "We're in the middle of an apocalypse, after all. We take a little ride, and later we'll go kick some more Islamist Zombie-ass."

Heartfelt thanks to all who have supported me during the publishing process of this novella, especially my wonderful crew: Ingo, Michael, Sylvia, Ilona, Janet, and my dear mother. In memoriam to my dear father, Fritz Krepinsky.

I also send a huge thank you to my Lovelybooks rounds! It's so great sharing with you!

In memoriam Franziska Pigulla, who has recited my novel *Spreeblut* with so much passion.

Best regards to everyone at *Goodies*, *Westberlin*, *Oslo*, *Kala*, and all the other Berlin cafés, where I hung out to write. SomaFM Dronezone is and will always be the best musical background when in my own home.

Like always I'm tremendously grateful to my readers, who have awarded me, an independent writer, with their trust. If you have questions or suggestions, please write to: info@nichtdiewelt.de.

Take care and stay safe!
Karsten Krepinsky

www.theworldbehindthewindow.com

The author

Karsten Krepinsky is a German author and lives in Berlin. He holds a PhD in biology. When not working for a start-up company in the field of neurosciences, his passion is to write mystery, sci-fi, and horror novels. A great source of inspiration to Karsten is the vibrant city of Berlin.

The translator

Karin Dufner, holder of an M.A. in American literature, has been working as a translator of fiction since 1989, seeing herself as a wanderer between the English and the German language. Her bibliography encompasses around 400 titles. Her ivory tower is located in the Düsseldorf area, Germany.

The cover designer

Ingo Krepinsky is co-founder and manager of the Bremen, Germany based design agency Die Typonauten. He studied communication design at the University of the Arts Bremen and the University of Applied Sciences and Arts Hannover. He has won several design contests such as *iF communication design award*, *The German Design Award* (nominated) or *Stiftung Buchkunst* (best designed books). The design performance and font work of Die Typonauten are consistently presented in international journals. The foundry was selected as German independent type foundry for *Typography, Referenced – A Comprehensive Visual Guide to the Language, History, and Practice of Typography*, a publication of Rockport Publishers.